MW01257162

Ice Cream Crime

By

J.M. Poole

Sign up for Jeffrey's newsletter to get all the latest corgi news— Click here AuthorJMPoole.com

BOOKS BY
JEFFREY M. POOLE

Cozy Mystery
CORGI CASE FILES
Case of the One-Eyed Tiger
Case of the Fleet-Footed Mummy
Case of the Holiday Hijinks
Case of the Pilfered Pooches
Case of the Muffin Murders
Case of the Chatty Roadrunner
Case of the Highland House Haunting
Case of the Ostentatious Otters
Case of the Dysfunctional Daredevils
Case of the Abandoned Bones
Case of the Great Cranberry Caper
Case of the Shady Shamrock
Case of the Ragin' Cajun
Case of the Missing Marine
Case of the Stuttering Parrot
Case of the Rusty Sword
Case of the Unlucky Emperor

Epic Fantasy
BAKKIAN CHRONICLES
The Prophecy
Insurrection
Amulet of Aria

(coming soon from Secret Staircase Books)

(coming soon from Secret Staircase Books)

CORGI CASE FILES

Case of the

Ice Cream Crime

Book 18

J.M. POOLE

Secret Staircase Books

Case of the Ice Cream Crime
Published by Secret Staircase Books, an imprint of
Columbine Publishing Group, LLC
PO Box 416, Angel Fire, NM 87710

Book layout and design by Secret Staircase Books
Ice Cream graphics in chapters by Dietmar Hoepfl Jun

First trade paperback edition: June, 2023
First e-book edition: June, 2023

* * *

Publisher's Cataloging-in-Publication Data

Poole, J.M.
Case of the Ice Cream Crime / by J.M. Poole.
p. cm.
ISBN 978-1649141408 (paperback)
ISBN 978-1649141415 (e-book)

1. Zachary Anderson (Fictitious character)—Fiction. 2.
Amateur sleuth—Fiction. 3. Pet detectives—Fiction. I. Title

Corgi Case Files Mystery Series : Book 18.
Poole, J.M., Corgi Case Files mysteries.

BISAC : FICTION / Mystery & Detective.

813/.54

CONTENTS

ACKNOWLEDGMENTS

There are always so many people to thank and acknowledge when writing a book. I know I'll usually leave a few off, so if I do, and you see that I haven't properly thanked you, don't hate me. First off, and I can't stress this enough, I have to thank my wife, Giliane. She and I were watching TV a few months back and, in the same sentence, we heard "ice cream" and "crime". She looked at me and said that'd make a great title for a book.

I also want to thank the members of my Posse. As always, you guys rock! My thanks goes out to Diane, Caryl, Jason, Louise, Carol, and Robin. Also, from Secret Staircase Books, I have to thank my beta readers: Sandra, Paula, Susan, Marcia, Isobel, and Brooke. Thank you!

With this book, I've taken a few liberties with business names and their locations around the Southern Oregon area. Some of the shops are based on real locations, others aren't. So, before you go checking the maps, or searching for them online, no, you're not going to be able to find any of them.

Finally, I want to extend my thanks to you, the reader. Thank you for keeping the interest alive in Zack and his dogs!

For Giliane — Always & forever, my dear.

Fifteen years, Zachary! For fifteen years, Cookbook Nook has never, *ever* been robbed. What in the world could they have wanted? I sell cookbooks! Well, cookbooks and kitchen appliances. But who'd want that so badly that they'd stoop to committing a felony? Vance didn't mention anything?"

"Not to me, he didn't," I said. "Rivendale?"

"No Middle Earth references. Du coeur?"

"What did you say? Duker? Nah."

We had just arrived home from our impromptu trip to Sitka, Alaska. Our last day in the Land of Midnight Sun ended with us receiving news that Jillian's store, located in our home of Pomme Valley, Oregon, had suffered a break-in. Vance Samuelson, senior detective on the local police force (and good friend), was the one who broke the news to us. As luck would have it, we were already on our way home.

The ride share dropped us off at Jillian's house, Carnation Cottage, one of a dozen historic houses in town. Our luggage was shoved out of the way as we hurriedly grabbed a set of car keys off a nearby hook and headed for the garage. I briefly considered leaving the dogs here, only Sherlock and Watson knew something was up and pointedly refused to leave our side.

Before I go any further, allow me to introduce myself. That is, if you aren't familiar with who we are. My name is Zack Anderson, and riding along with me in my Jeep is my lovely, albeit a touch furious wife, Jillian. I'm comfortably in my mid-forties, stand six feet tall, and as for weight? Well, let's just say I'm somewhere north of two hundred.

As I mentioned earlier, my wife and I are residents of a little city in southwest Oregon by the name of Pomme Valley, or PV for short. Our town is a mere ten minutes from Medford, and about forty-five minutes southeast from Grants Pass. I personally moved here a few years ago when, needing a drastic change of scenery from the scorching Arizona desert, I learned I had been given a large inheritance from my late wife's family, which involved a decent chunk of land. Instead of just selling it, which I will admit had been my first thought, I decided it might just be what I needed, and opted to uproot my entire life to leave behind everything I knew.

The welcome I received from the Pacific Northwest was less than friendly, and within twenty-four hours of stepping foot onto Oregonian soil, I found my sorry tail in jail, accused of murder. No, I wasn't guilty, but I will admit I couldn't fault the cops. After all, evidence linking me to the crime was everywhere. I won't bore you with the details, but thankfully, I discovered I had a friend in town. That'd be Harrison Watt, my best friend from high school. He had cleaned up his act, buckled down with his studies, and became a veterinarian. He was also the one who suckered me into adopting a dog.

And now a tri-colored corgi enters the scene.

Sherlock has to be, hands-down, the smartest dog I have ever encountered. That squat little dog somehow managed to sniff out the clues necessary to keep me from doing time. Whether it was something as trivial as a picture, or as insignificant as a piece of candy, Sherlock always managed to nudge me in the right direction. And, much to my surprise, he and I clicked right from the start. I never imagined myself a dog owner, but now? I can't imagine my life without him. Or her.

I adopted a second dog, thanks to Harry, yet again. She was also a Pembroke corgi, classified as red and white. Sherlock was already named when I got him, but for my sweet little girl, I decided on Watson.

No laughing, and no judging.

Watson, and I'm clueless as to how Sherlock pulled this off, learned how to notice clues from her packmate. Those two dogs are so gifted at solving crimes that the three of us were officially hired as police consultants for the PVPD. We've found missing artifacts, located hiding fugitives, and have rescued missing animals, which include

—we recently learned—those living in much colder climates than us. Vance told me a while ago that the corgis have successfully solved more cases than practically the entire police force, combined. I honestly don't think he minds, but I *have* been noticing derisive looks from PV cops whenever we see them.

By profession, I'm mostly known for my writing, penning romance novels under the name Chastity Wadsworth. I know, I know, it sounds an awful lot like a woman. At the recommendation of my first agent, and his insistence that women romance authors sell more than male authors do, I allowed him to come up with a name that he promised would sell books. True to his word, Chastity Wadsworth was a major hit. To be honest. I couldn't write the books fast enough. Everything with that name on the cover became an instant hit. The money started rolling in, I was able to easily pay the bills, and began investing money.

That was about the time that my former agent decided he wasn't getting a big enough share, and without my knowledge, began fudging the books. I, being the trusty sap that I was, refused to believe anything was wrong. Well, that came to a screeching halt when I was contacted by a few other authors he represented, and when we compared notes, we realized it was time to get the authorities involved. That's when my new agent and publisher, MCU, which is short for Manheim Company Unlimited, appeared on the scene. They promised honesty and an open-book policy that I found hard to believe. But, seeing as how I was between agents and publishers, I gave them a trial run.

That was more than ten years ago.

Man-Chest United, er, I mean, MCU, has taken very good care of me, so unless something dire happens, I don't plan on changing our arrangement anytime soon. Based on how much I get in royalties, I can only imagine they don't want to disturb their cash cow, either.

The final bit of explanation I find worth mentioning is that I'm a winery owner. I know I should've said I inherited a winery earlier, but did you know that Lentari Cellars is so well known in this area there are waiting lists just to get a bottle? Sure, I'd like to take credit, but I can't. My master vintner, Caden Burne, deserves responsibility for that. He has full say over everything that happens. New flavors, bottle and label design, equipment requests, and so on. The only thing I have to do is sign the checks whenever an invoice falls on my desk. Oh, and subject myself to taste-testing whenever the sadistic son of a biscuit eater wants to try out a new flavor on me. It's a well-known fact that I *detest* wine. Can't stand the sight, smell, or taste of the stuff.

Now back to our regularly scheduled programming.

We arrived at the outskirts of town, and I automatically eased my foot off the gas. Cookbook

Nook was situated in a large, purple building that it shared with a few smaller stores on either side of it. It wasn't until earlier this year that I found out Jillian owned the building. Then again, it wasn't surprising. Thanks to her late first husband, my darling wife will never have to work again. But has that stopped her? No. Having tons of money will sometimes bring out the worst in people, but I'm very thankful to say that it doesn't apply to Jillian. Not only that, but I also know she has secretly funded a bunch of her friends' businesses, on top of making huge donations to quite a few well-deserved charities. I'd also like to point out that I do quite well for myself, too, and while my bank account is nowhere near the size of hers, it's fairly significant.

Back to the problem at hand.

Right away, I noticed a couple of police cars parked in front of Jillian's store. With them was a very recognizable hunk of junk, namely Vance's Oldsmobile sedan. Crime scene tape was stretched across the door, and a sizeable crowd had gathered on the sidewalk, eagerly peering inside to see what was happening. I took the alley behind the store and parked my Jeep next to the back door. We had no sooner entered the store when we came face to face with Vance Samuelson.

"Zack! Jillian! What the—how did you get here so fast?"

I bumped fists with my detective friend. "Hey, Vance. I tried to tell you we were already on our way home. What's going on? How bad was the place hit?"

"See for yourself. Hi, Jillian. I'm sorry to have to show you this."

"Hello, Vance," Jillian returned. "I'm a big girl. Move aside. I want to see for myself what happened."

We emerged from the staff-only back room to find a good portion of the store in disarray. Racks had been tipped over. Books were strewn about the floor, like discarded trash. Several displays of local candles had been smashed, which prompted me to rein in the dogs. The last thing I needed to worry about was picking glass out of their paws.

"Oh, my. They made a mess, didn't they?"

The section of the store that was dedicated to kitchen gadgets hadn't fared any better. Spatulas, spoons, and tongs had been dumped onto the floor. Several of Jillian's larger appliances, the mixers and blenders, had been shoved off their shelves, too.

As I slowly turned to take in the damage, a small part of my brain woke up and started speaking to me, telling me something wasn't right. Something was off here, as if this whole mess was just a cover-up. However, this is just a kitchen store. What more could they have possibly wanted?

My eyes hit the stairs and slowly traveled upward. What about the second floor? Was it unscathed or had it befallen the same bad luck as the ground floor?

"It was hit, too," Vance remarked. "You're looking at the top floor? It wasn't spared, I'm afraid."

I heard Jillian sigh. I took her hand and gave it a reassuring squeeze.

"Don't you worry. We'll find out who did this. We'll get it all cleaned up."

Jillian leaned into my shoulder. "Thank you."

A clatter sounded on our left, and when we turned, we saw a large group of what appeared like high schoolers sitting, cross-legged, on the floor. From the looks of things, they were working to establish some sort of order to the chaos. I knew my wife categorized her cookbooks by type, and since I saw growing piles of similarly-themed titles forming in front of me, clearly someone had figured it'd be the easiest way to get product back on the shelves as quickly as possible.

A red-headed teenaged girl approached us. She smiled fleetingly at me before turning to Jillian. Surprisingly, it wasn't a look of dismay on her face but determination—resolve. Sherlock and Watson both looked up at Cookbook Nook's young manager and waggled their stumpy tails. The young girl threw her arms around my wife.

"Sydney, are you okay?" Jillian asked.

The store manager broke the hug and nodded. "I'm fine. I can't believe you're back! Oh, tell me you didn't cut your trip short because of this. It's only a mess. We'll have this cleaned up in no time. See? I brought some help." Sydney indicated a group of similarly aged boys and girls. "Guys, come here. You need to meet Mrs. Jillian Anderson. She's the owner here, and my boss. Mrs. Anderson, standing from left to right are Serena, Krissi, Beth, Pete, Dustin, and Lisa. They're friends of mine from school, who are all seniors now. Back there, sorting books, are Tami, Erik, David, and Cindi. Like me, they all graduated this year. They're helping me clean up."

I looked at Vance. "Is that okay? Have the crime scene techs gone through here?"

"Our boys finished with the place several hours ago," Vance confirmed. "The front door was smashed open. The register was forced, too, and is empty. I think this was just a simple smash and grab."

Sydney looked up. "I don't think it was."

"Do you know something we don't?" Vance asked. He pulled his notebook from his inner pocket and clicked his pen, indicating he was ready to take a statement.

"Just a feeling, I guess. It looks like whoever did this tried to create as much of a mess as possible. If they wanted something, why didn't they just take it and run?"

I nodded. "I couldn't agree more. I can't shake the feeling that something's not right."

"I just wish I could've been here," Sydney moaned.

"The only thing that would've accomplished is getting yourself hurt," I told the girl. "You have no idea if our perp was armed."

"I've been taking self-defense classes," Sydney proudly proclaimed. "I could've gone all Hong Kong Phooey on them. It'd serve them right."

"How does a girl your age even know who Hong Kong Phooey is?" I wanted to know. Respect for Jillian's manager rose several notches higher. "Fantastic cartoon, by the way."

"There's a channel on TV that plays all the oldies," I was told.

Sighing, I gave the girl a smile. "Oldies. That's just great. Well, as disturbing as that is, I'll let it go."

I suddenly noticed Vance look up at the ceiling.

"I've been meaning to ask you guys something. Jillian, don't you have this place protected?"

"There are nearly a dozen cameras in my store," Jillian confirmed, "covering every angle in here. Just because you can't see them doesn't mean they aren't there."

"Music to my ears. Any chance I could get you to pull up the footage from … I guess it'd be last night through this morning?"

Jillian nodded. "Of course. The terminal is in my office upstairs. If you'll excuse me?"

"I'm sorry I had to call you back, pal," Vance said, the moment Jillian had gone. "I figured that, if ever there was someone who could protect what's hers, it'd be Jillian. I may not have seen the cameras, but I just *knew* they were here. Wow. I'm looking for them and I still don't see any. Do you?"

I pointed straight up. "I'm guessing there's one right there."

"What, the smoke detector? You think there's a camera on it?"

"Well, look at it. Does that look like a smoke detector to you?"

"Well, yeah, I guess."

"Look around, pal. Those circular gizmos are everywhere. Plus, I don't see any test buttons on them, or flashing red lights. In fact, look over there. See that one on the wall, near the exit sign? I just saw a flash of red. *That* is a smoke detector. As for all those other things? I'm guessing they're part of some sophisticated security system. I wouldn't be surprised if that giant hockey puck up there has infrared cameras, motion-tracking cameras, and probably high-tech microphones."

"Huh. Who knew, right? Hey, how'd it go in Alaska? Must be nice to get free trips everywhere!"

"Did you, or did you not, accompany us to New Orleans for that book signing?" I reminded my friend. "All expenses paid. Remember scoring yourself that souvenir jazz program you presently have framed and on your wall? Signed by Louis Armstrong? Any of this ring a bell?"

"Yeah, yeah, you make a good point. What happened up north? Did you and the dogs have to do something there?"

"Remember what I told you happened in Monterey?" I countered. When Vance nodded, I continued. "The guy in charge apparently talked to the people at CCCP, and our names were mentioned. Monterey Bay Aquarium was so impressed with us that they advised their Alaskan friends to bring us to Sitka to see if we could locate a stolen penguin chick."

"Man, someone took off with a baby penguin? How uncool is that?"

"No worries. We took care of everything."

"Zachary?" Jillian called from upstairs. "Could you come up here, please?"

There was something about her tone that had me looking for someone who could take control of my dogs. As if by magic, Sydney appeared by my side and held out a hand. Nodding appreciatively at the girl, I passed her Sherlock and Watson's leashes. Not sure what to expect, I took the stairs two at a time and hurried to my wife's side. However, one didn't need to be a forensic expert to know what was bothering her.

The upstairs was even more of a mess than down below. Whoever did this had a great time rearranging the furniture, and by that, I mean pushing things over, sliding chairs across the floor, and knocking things off their shelves. However, Jillian wasn't even looking at any of that. She was in the café, standing before a trashed display case. I don't mean the glass case had taken physical damage. Standing next to Jillian, I saw what had happened. Someone had a great time pulling out various bits of food, sampling them, and then returning the uneaten portions. Glancing at the second glass case, I was surprised to see what was in it.

"Since when have you started serving ice cream?" I asked.

"This was installed just a few days before we left for Alaska. I had been thinking about expanding the café for a while now. I guess you could say that I was inspired by my meeting with Sonya Ladd."

"Who's Sonya Ladd?" I wanted to know.

"She's a new friend I met in Ashland. She makes her own organic ice cream and has come up with some wonderful recipes. She had it available to sample in her kitchen and I have to tell you I was blown away by it. If I knew it hadn't been contaminated, I'd give you a sample. As it is, based on the severity of the mess up here, I think it needs to be tossed."

"What a waste," I sighed.

She pointed out one in particular. The ice cream in the tub was white and included several ribbons of different color. According to the name placard next to the title, this flavor was a Tahitian vanilla base with a ribbon of strawberry puree and chunks of kiwi and raspberries. And the name —*Celebration*. The second flavor, however, was a mystery. Why? It was missing. *That* is why my wife called me upstairs.

"I see the second name tag. Our perp stole ice cream? How hungry was this guy, anyway?"

According to the sign, the missing tub

contained a flavor called *Hawaiian Sunrise*. It is a strawberry sorbet swirled with a ribbon of pineapple puree, sprinkled with white coconut flakes. Wow. And here I thought I was a true ice cream aficionado by preferring French vanilla to just basic vanilla. Whoever created those flavors was way more creative than I am.

"Ice cream. The guy stole your ice cream. Why wouldn't he take the other one?" I asked. "Personally, I think it sounds better than this sunrise one, but then again, I'm a fan of vanilla. Plus, the only place pineapple belongs is on a pizza."

"Don't even get me started with pineapple on a pizza," Jillian warned, wagging a finger at me. "You can't beat fresh pineapple, and that's what Sonya used in her recipe. I just can't believe someone took the whole tub."

I swung my arm in a circle, encompassing the surrounding area. "You're not suggesting ice cream was what this guy was after, are you? Who in the world would break into a business just to steal some dessert?"

"It does seem silly once you say it out loud, doesn't it?"

I shrugged. "Stranger things have happened. Take the Grinch, who broke into houses that one Christmas. He only wanted the presents and nothing else. So, it doesn't really surprise me too much that this guy wanted the entire tub of this specialty ice cream."

"The entire tub," Jillian repeated. Her brow furrowed and she looked over at the counter. "I wonder."

"You wonder *what*?" I asked.

"I need to check my freezer. I was able to buy both tubs of that flavor, which is all Ms. Ladd had to sell."

"Makes sense. Huh. You learn something new each day. I didn't think there was enough room back there to store a freezer."

"Actually, there *is* one just behind the counter, but it's only a small chest model. If I'd had this building built from the ground up, then I would have had a full sized one installed. As it stands, there wasn't any way to get a walk-in freezer on the second floor. So, the main one is downstairs. Will you help me?"

"Of course. Lead the way."

We trooped back down the stairs and saw that Sydney's team of fellow students was doing a fantastic job cleaning up the mess. Four girls were making sure the books ended up on the right bookcases. Two others were straightening and vacuuming. The boys were busy returning order to the kitchen appliances. As for Sydney, she was behind the counter, working on reattaching all the cables for the computer-based cash registers. Sherlock and Watson were sharing a recliner as they watched the proceedings. Sydney looked up as we descended. One glance at Jillian's face had her hurrying around the counter.

"Mrs. Anderson? Is everything okay? I'm sorry to say I haven't had a chance to go upstairs yet."

"It's actually worse than here," Jillian confided. "Don't worry about that for now. I need to check the freezer."

"Is she doing okay?" Sydney whispered to me, as Jillian hurried off.

I shrugged. "She's doing pretty good, all things considered. Me? I would have been severely ticked off. The first thing Jillian said to me, after we boarded the plane in Alaska, was that she hoped everyone was all right. She didn't want to see anyone get hurt."

"Someone would have been hurt had I been here," Sydney said, frowning.

I grinned at the girl. "It's good that you stand up for yourself, but just be careful, okay? Nothing is worth risking your life."

"That's easy for you to say, Mr. Anderson. You're a big guy. You can easily scare someone away. As for me, people take one look at me and just assume I scream like a … well, like a girl, and turn to putty. Well, okay, to be honest, that would have been me a few months ago. Now, I believe I can stand up for myself and dare anyone to say otherwise."

I held up a fist and waited for her to bump it with her own.

Jillian appeared, and if possible, seemed more perturbed than before. "They took it! It's gone, too!"

"What, that other tub of *Celebration*?" I asked.

Sydney looked up. "Ice cream? They took your ice cream? Ooo, that infuriates me to no end."

"Take it down a notch, She-Ra," I told her, which earned me a giggle from both ladies present. "Stranger things have happened. Did you have any luck with the security footage?"

My wife's mouth dropped open. "Oh, I completely forgot. I saw the café and forgot that I was headed to my office. I'll go there now."

"I'll take the dogs through the store and see if they pick up anything."

Jillian nodded. "That's a good idea. Vance, will you go with him?"

Vance nodded. "Ordinarily, I'd say he'd be fine by himself, but seeing how I wasn't expecting you guys to arrive home just yet, I'll take advantage of the situation and tag along."

"Watch out for broken glass," Jillian warned, as she ascended the steps once more.

Having heard their names, Sherlock and Watson jumped down from the armchair, sniffed noses, and then looked back at me, as though they were confused why they were here.

"There's a bad guy out there," I began, "who has caused your mommy a great deal of work."

"Your daddy, too," Vance added.

"Right, so we need to cheer her up. Would you two like to look around? If there's something in here we need to know about, now's the time to point it out, okay?"

Sherlock gave himself a solid shake, causing his

collar to rattle like crazy. Watson stared at me for a few moments before dropping back to the floor and rolling over. I gave her a few belly rubs and before I could straighten up, the two of them were on their feet and tugging on their leashes.

"I'll take that as a good sign," Vance decided.

"I'd like to think so. Sherlock? Take point, buddy."

My tri-colored corgi dropped his nose to the ground and started sniffing. The two of us followed the dogs as they wove their way through the mess Cookbook Nook had become. Then again, Sydney and her friends were doing a remarkable job in restoring order. Aside from having just about everything dumped onto the floor, there was very minimal damage.

"Excuse us," I announced, as Sherlock nudged his way by several girls sitting cross-legged on the floor. The teens paused from their book sorting to look up. "Don't move, 'kay? We're heading *thataway*," I said, pointing toward the back right corner of the store.

"You're so lucky, Mr. Anderson," one of the girls gushed. "I love corgis!"

I smiled back at the girl and nodded. Sherlock, ignoring everything and everyone, continued to pull me in that direction. Once we got there, I noticed we were in a small section Jillian had deemed *Decorating*. There were books about fondant, gum paste, creating buttercream flowers, and so on. At least, those were the titles I could see on the floor.

Is that what the dogs wanted me to see? Books on cake decorating? One glance at the corgis, however, confirmed that it wasn't. Both of them were staring at a picture on the wall. Curious to see what it was, I joined them near the window and studied the image.

It was a print depicting an idyllic green meadow, with the edge of a forest visible in the distance. A small creek was there, winding its way around trees, boulders, and small hills. The sky was bright blue, with fluffy white clouds starting to dissipate. Taking center stage in the picture was a rainbow, falling from above and touching down on the meadow itself.

I could see why Jillian would hang such a picture in her store. I felt myself relaxing just by gazing at it. Wait. Is that what Sherlock and Watson were doing? Admiring the scenery?

My cell rang, and one look at the display had me shaking my head. "Jillian? What are you calling me for? Aren't you upstairs? Is everything okay?"

"Zachary, you need to see this."

"We'll be right there."

At least, that was the plan. Then again, neither corgi budged until I snapped a photo of the framed print. The moment I did, Sherlock and Watson were anxious to head upstairs. How they knew I needed to return to the second level, I'll never know.

"You're not going to believe this guy," my wife

said, as I entered her office, adjacent to the café. "He not only knew there were cameras in here, he made certain they caught him in the act!"

"Huh?" I stammered, confused. "He *wanted* to get caught stealing?"

I looked over Jillian's shoulder and watched the monitor on her desk. An image was currently frozen, showing the front entry and a man, dressed in a white tee shirt and dark pants, strolling through the front door. Bear in mind, this was after he used something to punch through the glass. Sledgehammer? Glass cutter? Maybe a rock? I couldn't tell, but then again, it wasn't important. What *was* important was the man on the screen. He wasn't wearing a mask or making any effort to hide his face.

"There's something you don't see every day," I said. "Do you recognize him?"

"No. Look at him. His hair's a mess, his shirt is torn, and he looks … dirty. If I didn't know any better, then I'd say we are looking at a homeless person."

I squinted at the screen. Jillian was right. The clothes were ragged, his face was covered with a scraggly beard, and he made no effort to hide from the cameras. This was someone, I decided, who had nothing to lose.

"It's only one person? What, did he spend the night in here? That's one mother of a mess for just a single person to make. Can you tell when he entered, and left?"

Jillian tapped away at her keyboard. "I should. Give me just a few moments."

I ducked out of the office to see if Vance was still here, which he was. He caught sight of me, standing at the top of the stairs, and headed over.

"Got anything for me?"

"That and then some," I reported. "The guy who did this appears to be a homeless dude, and he wasn't wearing a mask."

"Jillian has a clear shot of his face?"

I came thiiiiiiiiis close to correcting his grammar, in a proper Jillian-approved manner, but managed to catch myself in time. Inserting a *had* into the conversation just wasn't worth it at the moment.

"No mask, no hiding from the cameras, no nothing," I confirmed.

"Awesome. Let's head up. Wait, only one guy?"

"That's what I'm having her check," I told my friend. "If it was just him, then I asked her to find out just how long he spent in the store."

"Good thinking."

We both entered Jillian's office. My wife was waiting with an answer. "I've got him on video, holding both tubs of ice cream as he left."

Vance looked up. "Ice cream? He stole ice cream? You're kidding."

Jillian shook her head. "I'm not, I'm afraid. I found a tub missing at the café, and the second tub, which I had in the freezer downstairs, was also taken."

"That makes no sense," Vance quietly murmured. "Why would someone break in here just to steal ice cream?"

"We're wondering that ourselves," Jillian confessed.

"What time did he show up?" Vance asked.

"He got in sometime after midnight. I don't think he was the one who broke the front door. From the angle I have, it looks as though he was wandering by when he noticed the hole."

Vance's face hardened. "Do you recognize the guy?"

"No, I'm sorry."

"Can you tell what happened to the door? When did it break?"

Jillian tapped away on her keyboard. "I'm checking. There it is. It happened about twenty minutes before our thief found his way inside. It looks like something large and heavy struck the door. What that is, I cannot say."

"Does your system have a way to share footage, or could you save me a copy on a flash drive?" Vance asked.

Jillian resumed tapping on her keyboard. "I've got online access. I'll specify which files I want to share, and then send that link to you. All you'll have to do is click it, and the video will open."

"Thanks, Jillian. That's perfect. Zack, care to give me a hand?"

"You betcha." I gave my wife a kiss. "I'm going to check this out. Is there a camera outside, which covers the front?"

"There isn't, but there will be just as soon as I can get one ordered," Jillian vowed.

The two of us returned to the ground floor. Sherlock and Watson perked up and, seeing me, hurried over. Sydney nodded in my direction and returned to supervising her friends.

"You don't think this is a coincidence, do you?"

Vance shook his head. "Not at all. Someone *wanted* that transient to find his way inside. Or … whoever pulled this off gave the guy orders to get in here and have a field day. I just don't know where the ice cream fits in."

Sherlock rattled his collar and looked up at the two of us.

"What is it, boy?" I asked.

"Woof."

That got Vance's attention.

"Did you find something already? Good boy. You, too, Watson. What did you guys find?"

The corgis tugged on their leashes. We were led to the front of the store, where a makeshift plywood door had been set up. Sydney and her team had managed to sweep the glass to the side, so I didn't have to worry about Sherlock and Watson hurting their paws. However, both dogs stopped short of the makeshift door and sniffed the ground. Vance and I squatted to see what had attracted their attention. Something had hardened on the floor. Something white, like …

"Is that ice cream?" Vance asked, impressed.

"Good job, Sherlock. You, too, Watson. Okay, I owe you guys a couple of pizzle sticks."

If you have to ask what those are, let me warn you now. Don't. Some things are best left unsaid. If you *do* know what they are, then I know you'll sympathize with me.

"Oh, no you don't," I argued, waggling my finger. "Those damn things are disgusting, *and* they smell."

"Hey, you're not the ones eating them," Vance countered. "At least, I hope you're not."

"Ha ha, pal."

"Guys? Find the guy who stole that ice cream and I'll buy you a dozen each of the pizzle sticks *and* pig ears."

"You're just trying to gross me out, aren't you?" I complained.

The corgis perked up. They shared a look and headed outside. Both turned left and we found ourselves marching along Main Street. The dogs hesitated as another drip was discovered. At least, I assumed it was. Sherlock and Watson both sniffed a white smudge the size of a dime, looked at us, and then proceeded on their way.

"We're getting quite a few looks," Vance remarked, as he fell into step beside me and the dogs. "You'd think I'd be used to it by now."

Passing motorists were slowing their cars and rolling their windows down. People shouted my dogs' names as they passed us by. Sherlock and Watson, for the record, didn't bother looking up.

Apparently, they were too fixated with following the trail of dried ice cream.

We crossed Main and approached Oregon Street. The dogs turned right, so we did the same. Had they lost the trail? After all, another ten minutes of walking brought us to the police station. Try as I might, I just couldn't imagine our perp waltzing into the police station to share his ill-gotten treats.

The dogs veered again. This time, we headed north, toward a residential neighborhood, but as we neared, the trail changed again. Now it looked as though … what the heck was this guy doing? Heading back to town? That left me no choice but to assume the trail we were following was left by an idiot. Hmm. Or maybe a drunk, holding two tubs of melting ice cream. I dismissed the notion and sighed. That couldn't be right.

Before I knew it, we were back on Main Street, only this time, we were on the opposite side with Sherlock, sniffing like mad as we walked, ducking between two businesses and heading for the narrow alley running between the shops. I could tell that he was making a beeline straight for the closest dumpster.

Vance was shaking his head.

"What, he steals the ice cream and then tosses it? What's the logic in that?"

"Nothing about this makes sense so far," I decided. When Sherlock and Watson both sat next to the dumpster, I shrugged and reached for the lid. "I'm starting to think the guy was paid to do it. He ... *holy crap!*"

Vance shoved me out of the way and drew his gun.

"What is it? What do you ... oh." The gun was holstered. "Well, that doesn't help us much, does it?"

Inside the dumpster, looking at us with dull, lifeless eyes was the man from the video. Also worth noting was the absence of the ice cream. More confused than ever, I shared a look with my detective friend.

"Any suggestions?"

"Not a one, buddy."

Two uneventful days passed. Curiosity getting the better of me, I checked in with Vance several times in those forty-eight hours, hoping to hear an update on our unidentified John Doe. However, the poor fellow hadn't been carrying any ID, and his fingerprints were not in any accessible database. Vance assured me he was doing everything he could to get a positive identification, but until that happened, there really wasn't anything else for me to do.

Our contractor had called, indicating he had a few questions for us about our new house we were having built, so Jillian and I, along with the dogs, stopped by to see what he wanted.

"It's coming along nicely!" Jillian exclaimed, as we stepped out of the car. "What about calling it Lilac House?"

"You already have Carnation Cottage. No flowers."

"Spoilsport. Well? What's your suggestion?"

"Hmm. Coruscant?"

"The Star Wars planet that's just a great big city? No, thank you."

I set both dogs on the ground and headed toward the individual wearing a blue flannel shirt, jeans, and heavy work boots. A bright yellow hard hat was perched atop his head, although it looked like it would tip too far forward at any moment and slide off. A pair of ripped leather gloves completed his outfit.

Chuck Whiteson was slightly older than me, making him in his late forties. He had prematurely gray hair and a thick handlebar moustache; he was loud, boisterous, and probably the friendliest contractor I have ever encountered. And naturally, he was a good friend of Jillian's. Actually, I think he's a friend of her father's, but that didn't matter to me. The guy is probably one of those people who could be dropped into the middle of a jungle and, a week later, be found in a hand-built, three-story bamboo tree house *with* running water. He knew his trade and didn't hesitate to let others know it.

"Did I read this right?" Chuck began, as we approached. "There's a stage in your theater room? Movie rooms I get, but a stage? Do I want to know why? You know what, scratch that. It's none of my business."

"It's for all the times we feel like reciting our favorite Shakespearean quotations," Jillian smoothly returned, not batting an eye.

Chuck's mouth fell open. He looked at me, certain he had heard that wrong. I shrugged helplessly.

"To be, or not to be? She's pulling your leg,

Chuck." I turned to Jillian. "You are, aren't you?"

My wife gave the foreman a smile. "Did you have a question about the stage, Chuck?"

"Well, yeah, I guess. Look, these plans call for something called a thrust stage."

Jillian nodded. "That's right."

Chuck sighed. "Could you … would you tell me what that's supposed to look like?"

"A thrust stage," Jillian began, "is a classification of stage where it's pushed out, among the audience."

"What's the purpose of that?" I asked, confused.

"It allows the audience to get as close as possible to the performers," my wife explained. "It's where people will typically surround the stage on three sides."

"And that's something you want?" I asked.

I could see that Jillian was about to answer in the affirmative, but then hesitated. "To tell the truth, I'm starting to wonder if thrust is what I really want."

The juvenile male still residing deep within my subconscious sniggered at the suggestion, which forced me to smile and look away. Jillian noticed and elbowed me in the stomach.

"Anyway," my wife continued, giving me a mischievous look, "I was thinking of switching the style to proscenium. Zachary, what do you think?"

"I think I need a dictionary," I remarked, drawing a grunt of agreement from Chuck. "Thrust? Proscenium? Care to enlighten us what those are?"

"They're just a few of the different stage designs," Jillian explained. "I already described a thrust stage. I can think of several others: proscenium, arena, and studio. Proscenium is probably the most common. You know the type, a large auditorium with a stage directly in front. They are usually sloped away from the audience."

I nodded. "And a thrust stage? Give me an example of that."

"Please," Jillian added, giving me a slight frown.

"Please," I quickly amended.

Chuck snapped his fingers. "Concerts! The stage sometimes juts out, into the audience."

My wife flashed our foreman a dazzling smile. "Yes, exactly!"

"An arena stage," I said, thinking hard. "Like, sporting events? Boxing, or wrestling?"

"I never knew those were considered stages," Chuck admitted.

"The other type I can think of is studio," Jillian said, alternating her look between the two of us. Consequently, her unrelenting look had me and Chuck fidgeting from foot to foot, like errant schoolboys. "Can either of you give me an example?"

"Studio," Chuck repeated. He eventually shrugged. "I don't think I know of any."

Jillian turned to me. "Zachary?"

I shrugged, and I'm sure I had a look on my face which said *I've got nothing*. "No, sorry."

"They're smaller," my wife explained, "more intimate. Think of a small room with a few rows of seats on several sides. The stage would be the ground floor, which is the same level as the first row of seats."

"And that's what you want here?" I asked, more confused than ever.

"No, I think I'll go with proscenium please, Chuck."

Our foreman was holding his phone and tapping the screen. After a few moments, his face lit up.

"Oh! I get it. It's more of a traditional setting, with the … I know what you want. I'll get on it, Mrs. Anderson."

"Thank you. Is there anything else we need to know about?"

"Only what I told you before, namely that the price of steel has increased. I'm sorry, there's no way to say that without coming across as greedy."

"You don't control the prices," Jillian said. "It'll be fine. Consider us informed."

Chuck wandered off. We watched the crew for a few moments as they scurried over all three levels of our huge house. The framing was finally up, electrical and plumbing appeared to be in place, and I was told the guy who sprays that expanding foam insulation should be here today. Scaffolding had been erected both outside and inside the house, and workers were scurrying over the structure like ants on an anthill. The roof was set to be sheathed by the end of the week, and the actual roof in the next week or so. I know Chuck was worried about Mother Nature, who up until this point, had been a royal pain in the … but, I digress. I trusted our foreman to do his job, and if he had to pull workers from one project to focus on completing another before a rainstorm could happen, then so be it.

My cell rang. I saw who was calling and put it on speaker.

"Hey, Vance. I was beginning to think you'd forgotten about me."

"Not much chance of that when you call every hour, on the hour."

"You told me the call this morning was only the second time you called," Jillian accused.

"Hah," Vance scoffed. "Not likely. Try the twentieth."

"Over-exaggerator," I laughed.

"Are you guys at the winery?"

"We're both here," I confirmed. "What's up? Are you headed this way?"

"I am. In fact, I'm just pulling in."

We watched Vance's Oldsmobile sedan enter our driveway and park next to my Jeep. Sherlock and Watson began pulling on the leashes even before Vance had shut off the engine.

"Brown nosers," I said. "I'm sure he hasn't forgotten to bring the treats. Give him a few moments. See? He's headed our way."

The corgis were pulling so hard that I was

briefly worried they'd hurt themselves. Making sure my friend was watching, I let go of both leashes. Having done this move quite a few times in the past, Vance snagged both leashes as soon as they were within range. He gave each of them a doggie biscuit—from the never-ending supply in his pocket—and walked them back to us.

"Hey, pal," I greeted, reclaiming the dogs' leashes. "I assume you've got some news for us about the dead guy?"

"He's been identified," Vance said, nodding. He pulled out his notebook. "Richard Hansen, sixty-seven. He was born in Sacramento, California, but how he ended up in Oregon, it doesn't say."

"What do we know about him?" Jillian wanted to know.

Vance consulted his notes. "Let's see. He had a drafting business, which tanked during the recession. He lost his business, his home, and his wife."

"He was paid to pull off that heist," I decided. "Someone learned about poor Richard's money troubles and then cast him aside, like nothing more than a piece of garbage. I've gotta tell you, that really ticks me off."

"You and me both, pal," Vance assured me. "Finding the person who did this has become top priority for everyone. The captain wants this case solved *yesterday*. Therefore, I'm officially calling in my team of consultants."

Sherlock and Watson looked up at my friend.

Both shook their collars and signaled their readiness.

"Where do you want to start?" I asked.

"You guys should head back to Jillian's store," Vance suggested. "Let the dogs roam. There might be something we missed."

"You got it. I'll let you know if they find anything. Hey, wait up. How did you determine Richard's identity? Were you able to track down any family members?"

My detective friend shook his head. "Nope. I mean, I tried. We found out he had a wife, but she's no longer in the area. She ended up moving to New Mexico and getting remarried. She wanted nothing to do with him and didn't even sound sad he was dead."

"How sad," Jillian commented.

"Did you find someone who knew him?" I asked.

Vance nodded. "You could say that. I showed his picture to a few other homeless people in town. Several said they knew him. Once they were properly motivated, so to speak, they told me everything I needed to know about Mr. Hansen."

"Cash," I said, nodding. "I didn't know the police did that."

"I didn't offer money," Vance corrected. "I stopped giving money to homeless people a long time ago."

"They don't deserve to go hungry," Jillian said, frowning. "You can't hold their situation against them."

Vance held up his hands in a time-out gesture.

"I said I didn't give them cash. I didn't say I refrained from giving them anything."

"Food," I guessed.

"Correctamundo," Vance said. "Gift cards, to be precise. I usually carry a number of food gift cards with me. That way, I know they'll be redeemed for food, and not something illegal."

"Food gift cards," I repeated, nodding. "That's a really good idea. I think I'll go out and pick some up."

"What for?" Vance asked.

"This case. We have a dead homeless guy. There's always a chance that I'll have to talk to some of them. It'd be good to have a selection on me, in case I need to do the same in order to get them to open up."

Jillian slipped her arm through mine. "That's very generous of you. I'll do the same."

"And blankets," I said, snapping my fingers. "It's been getting cold at night. I think I'll add some blankets, too. In fact, we ought to hold some type of event for them. Load them up with the necessary things they'll need to make it through next winter. Blankets, tents, jugs of water, etc."

"You are the sweetest," my wife gushed. "I'll match everything you do."

"Put me down for some, too," Vance said, as he returned to his car.

A second sweep of Cookbook Nook proved

inconclusive. The dogs weren't interested in anything. But, I will say that Sydney and her friends had done a wonderful job in restoring order to Jillian's store. With the exception of the plywood front door, it almost looked like nothing had happened. The café had its furniture righted and placed back in the seating area. In fact, several tables were occupied, as customers indulged in pastries, hot beverages, and whatever else was offered for sale in the glass display cases. Replacement tubs of ice cream beckoned invitingly, but before I could wander over to take a look, the dogs pulled me back to the stairs. Apparently, there was nothing up here for them to investigate, so they wanted to leave.

"Nothing?" Jillian asked.

"Not a thing," I confirmed. "They took one look at the order of the place and headed for the stairs. By the way, you can tell Sydney that she and her friends do amazing work. Makes me think that I ought to do something for them."

"I'm way ahead of you. I've already reached out to her and told her that this Friday, pizza is on me for her and her friends at Sara's Pizza Parlor. It's the least I could do."

We wandered over to several recliners when a commotion sounded from outside. The door opened and a steady stream of kids—all about the age of twelve—entered. The group of twenty kids immediately fanned out, heading to all four corners of the store.

"Stick with your buddy," a woman ordered. "No one is to go anywhere by themselves, is that clear?"

"Yes, Mrs. Needlemeyer," twenty children echoed.

"Dana!" Jillian exclaimed. "How nice to see you!"

The teacher, who was about the same age as me, turned to see my wife approach and broke out into a smile. "Jillian! We were hoping to see you today!"

"What brings you to my store?" I heard my wife ask.

"I'm giving the students a reward," the teacher confided. "Not one of them has missed any classes for the entire semester, and as such, I've told them that they can pick out anything five dollars and under. It'll be on me, of course."

"Of course it *won't*," Jillian argued. "To see that many students all smiling *and* wanting to come to class? You're in my store, therefore, I'll be picking up the tab."

"This is my idea, missy," Mrs. Needlemeyer argued. "You can … oh, this must be your husband. Dana Needlemeyer. And you're Zachary Anderson? Oh. Oh! Look! It's Sherlock and Watson!"

I had my hand out for a traditional handshake when I was promptly forgotten. The corgis, however, competed with each other to see who could make it to the school teacher first. Sighing, I dropped my hand. The dogs would always be more famous than I. You'd think I'd be used to it by now.

"They're so adorable! Look how friendly they

are!"

"They think you have treats," I clarified, as I gave each of my dogs a condescending look. Sherlock, to prove me wrong, rolled onto his back and waited for belly rubs. "You'd think I keep them kenneled at all hours of the day."

Dana squatted and was scratching Sherlock's stomach. Watson noticed the attention and immediately mimicked her packmate.

"This doesn't change anything," Dana mock-warned, as she tried to give Jillian a stern look. "I'm still paying for everything."

"Like you have a choice," Jillian laughed.

Several of the kids wandered into view, saw the dogs, and asked if they could pet them, too. I had just given permission when both corgis did this half-twist type of move and were on their feet in the blink of an eye. Both of them eyed the three kids who were approaching. Then, in unison, they turned to watch a bespectacled girl walk by. Several others appeared and were ignored. Then a boy holding a large bamboo spoon appeared, and the dogs' attention shifted to the newcomer.

I was still able to see the first kid they had fixated on perusing the shelves at the back of the store. I then compared the girl to the boy and could only come up with one similarity.

"What are they staring at?" Jillian wanted to know.

"Backpacks," I reported. I pulled out my cell just as two boys passed us. Both were wearing them, and both, I might add, were ignored. "Hmm, at least I *think* they're checking out their bags. Whatever. Look, guys. I'm taking their picture. Happy?"

They were. The kids were ignored, and both corgis went back to wanting more belly rubs. Dana, having no idea what had just transpired, smiled patronizingly at us, as though we had spoiled the dogs rotten, and clearly this is what Sherlock and Watson now expected. Hearing an argument break out from somewhere in the store, the teacher excused herself and moved off.

The next thing I knew, the serenity of the store was shattered by popular '80s music group Twisted Sister, belting out their most popular hit, *We're Not Gonna Take It*. That particular song had been assigned to only one of my contacts, and it wasn't hard to figure out who.

"Hey, Vance. I'm guessing you want an update? No problem. We walked up and down the ... what's that? Hold on. Let me put you on speaker. Okay, go ahead."

"He's younger than Richard," Vance was saying. "He and his family live in an apartment in Medford."

"What's going on?" Jillian asked, confused.

"Our dead guy has a brother," I relayed. "Vance found him. Have you talked to him yet?"

"I haven't. I'm on my way out there right now. I'm hoping the brother can shed some light on Richard's mental state."

"Do you need us to tag along?" I asked. I hadn't acted as a professional police consultant in a while, and I have to admit, the discovery of Richard Hansen in the dumpster had made me somewhat wary of what else we might find. "I've got the dogs with me."

"You know what? I think I can handle this one. I'm guessing the brother will confirm Richard was mentally unstable, and this will all be chalked up to being in the wrong place at the wrong time."

"If you change your mind, you know where to find me," I said.

"You got it, pal."

Once the call had been terminated, I pulled Jillian over to the recliners and indicated we should sit down.

"Is something on your mind?" Jillian inquired.

I held up my phone and waggled it. "I sent out a couple of feeler texts," I began. "I asked ..."

"Feeler texts?" my wife interrupted. "You're getting ready to ask someone for a favor?"

I nodded. "As a matter of fact, I am. Quite a lot of favors, actually. And thus far, I've received nothing but positive comments. I think we can really make a difference."

"Make a difference with *what*?" Jillian asked.

"This winter. Remember you said you'd match me with whatever I can pull together?"

"Of course. Wait. What are you planning?"

"Harry's on board, as are Dottie, Woody, Hannah, Taylor, and pretty much everyone else who's a contact in my phone. I'm thinking I'd like to hold an event here next week, out on the sidewalk on both sides of Main. All the business owners have agreed to pool their resources and bring tables and chairs. Come on, let me show you."

I took Jillian's hand and pulled her to her feet. Together, we walked outside. The skies were overcast, but it wasn't raining. The seasonal rains were due to pick up in the next couple of weeks or so. At the moment, it was probably in the low sixties outside, and quite pleasant. However, that stopped at sunset, when the temps would dip into the upper thirties once the sun excused itself for the night.

"If we set up some folding tables here and here, and if Hannah from Apple Blossom puts several tables just over there, then we can use them to set out coats, hats, scarves, and so on. I figure we can make this entire section of sidewalk all about winter wear."

I wasn't looking my wife in the eyes. If I had been, then I would have seen them fill with tears. It's also the time I checked the weather forecast on my phone and saw that the forecast had changed, and the freezing temps were now going to put in an appearance tomorrow night. Making a decision, I brought up my group chat I had instigated earlier — a skill I learned from Jillian — and inquired about upping the timeline. Within moments, I had everyone's permission and encouragement. Not one person told me no.

Man, I love this town.

"Change of plan," I said, as I took Jillian's hand. "Thanks to tomorrow night's forecast, we're going to hold our event tomorrow afternoon. I asked people to bring their folding tables, display racks, and anything they had lying around. We're gonna make this a party. I'll place calls to Sara's Pizza Parlor, and El Lonely Gringo, to see about getting some food brought over, too. That's on top of the gift cards I'm going to be picking up later. What? Too much?"

My wife pulled me in for a hug. "Not at all. Don't you ever change, Zachary."

Hannah chose that time to exit her store. PV's only floral shop was adjacent to Cookbook Nook, so I figured she must've seen the two of us out here. Plus, she had her phone in her hand.

"We're doing this tomorrow? That's perfect. Colin has the day off. He can help me set things up."

"Didn't he just have a day off last week?" Jillian asked.

Hannah held up a hand with two fingers displayed. "Two weeks ago, and yes, he did. Where were all these off days when we were in school? Oh, Zack. Thank you for setting all of this up. I know the people will love it."

I shrugged. "Everyone is so eager to donate their time or skills, that I needed something I could contribute. I mean, let's face it. I'm not gonna be handing out bottles of wine, right?"

Once more, the dulcet tones of heavy metal rock music assailed the senses. I hastily fumbled for my phone and offered the ladies a sheepish smile.

"Hey Vance, that was quick. I'm hoping you … what? You found *what*?"

Alarmed by the tone of my voice, both Jillian and Hannah fell silent. Even Sherlock and Watson turned to watch me as I started to pace.

"No, you're right. It's not good, it's bad. It has to be related, doesn't it? Right. Yep, I'll let everyone here know. Thanks, pal. Watch yourself out there."

"What was that all about?" Jillian asked, as I hung up the phone.

"The brother Vance mentioned earlier? Well, they found him all right: dead as a door nail."

THREE

An hour later, Sherlock, Watson, and I found ourselves in Medford, the next town over. I had arranged to meet Vance at the scene of the crime, which in this case, was a small, run-down apartment in a part of town I typically avoided. True to his word, Vance had officially requested help from his 'number one consultant', so here we were.

The corgis were off, the moment their feet hit the ground. Sherlock and Watson navigated around trash cans, a bike rack so bent and twisted that it could be loosely called art, and an old Dodge pickup truck that looked like it hadn't started in years. The dogs ducked between two buildings and headed for a rickety set of stairs next to a third. I noticed several of the stone steps were cracked. Thankfully, it was still serviceable.

Vance appeared at the top of the stairs. "Zack. Glad to see you, buddy. Hi Sherlock! How are you, boy? Watson. Lookin' as purty as ever!" Vance pulled two treats from his pocket and fed them to the dogs. "I'm actually glad you are a little bit late.

I was only given permission to inspect the scene about ten minutes ago."

"Huh? Really? Can I ask why?"

Vance motioned me close and dropped his voice. "The Medford police aren't too keen about letting us in there. Looks like they might be a bit jealous of the attention we've been getting lately. I personally think they don't want to be shown up by your dogs."

"Even if we can help them solve a murder that happened on their own turf?" I asked, growing incredulous.

"Keep your voice down. I think there might be someone still inside."

"MPD is still here?"

"They were adamant about checking *everything* before giving us access. So, are you ready? You've got your nose plugs with you, right? Grab a mop and follow me."

I'm sure my face paled. "You can't be serious."

"Of course, I'm not. Come on. I'll show you the scene."

"That's not cool, dude. Not cool at all."

"The look on your face made it worth it," Vance chuckled, as he opened the door to apartment 3B and lifted the yellow crime scene tape. "Next time, I need to remember to take a couple of pictures."

"Ha ha. So, what do we know about this guy?"

Vance consulted his notes. "His name was Matt. Let's see. Matthew Hansen, aged fifty-five, born in La Mirada, California, and lived most of his life there. From what I was told, he moved to Oregon less than five years ago."

"Didn't you tell me he and his family lived here?" I asked.

"Yeah, what about it?"

I slowly turned as I inspected the tiny, unkempt living space. "Well, look at this place. Does it look like a woman lives here?"

"One could," Vance insisted. "We won't know until we do a thorough examination of the place. Huh. You may be right. I'm surprised no one has said anything about that yet. Well, are you and the dogs ready to take a look?"

I nodded. "You bet. Wow, this place is a dump. We're both married, so we both know that a woman will typically not let her house get like this. No clothes, pieces of makeup, hairbrushes, or nail files. There are no signs there's anyone here but Matthew. See the shoes by the door? They're all the same size, and they all show about the same amount of wear." I strode to the entry closet and checked inside, but not before I caught the pair of latex gloves Vance tossed me. "A couple of sweatshirts and one heavy coat. Again, nothing that a woman couldn't wear, but I'm willing to wager that one doesn't."

Vance turned as one of the Medford crime scene techs wandered by, heading for the door.

"Looks like they're still here after all. Excuse me? Could you tell me where Mrs. Hansen is? Have we heard from her yet?"

"There isn't one," the tech insisted. "There was only Mr. Hansen."

"I was told he was married and that he lived here with his family," Vance argued.

The Medford technician shrugged. "Don't know what to tell you. Come to think of it, I seem to recall hearing the same thing. The only thing I can tell you is that I haven't seen any indications anyone but a slob lives here. If he has a family, then they live somewhere else. Take it from a guy who's been married for over fifteen years: our victim is a confirmed bachelor."

Nodding, I looked around the small living room, with the sagging couch, the squat two-shelf bookcase serving as the entertainment center, and the small secondhand flat panel television sitting on top. The dogs and I wandered over to the kitchen. Stacks of dirty dishes were in the sink, and there were fast food wrappers, empty pizza boxes, and take-out containers strewn across the counter. Steeling myself, I opened the fridge. Inside, I found a carton of moldy strawberries, a half-full quart of milk, a practically empty jar of grape jelly, and something sitting under a film of plastic wrap that had so much mold on it that I couldn't figure out what it was or used to be.

"Definitely single. Or divorced." I snapped my fingers. "Pictures."

Vance looked over at me. "Huh?"

"Photographs. If we really want to know whether or not he has kids, or maybe if he's separated and wants to reconcile with his wife, then don't you think there'd be pictures of them?"

Vance was silent as he considered. After a few moments, he glanced around the living room, then disappeared into the apartment's one bedroom. Several minutes later, he reappeared. "That was a good idea. I did find one picture. Check it out. It's him and I'm guessing his kids. They look like they're old enough to be in college."

"At fifty-five, that's totally possible. I keep thinking that, if I'd had kids back, let's say right out of high school, or college, then I could be old enough to be a grandfather now."

My friend snorted with amusement. "Does that bother you?"

I shrugged. "I guess it could, but it really doesn't. I'm happy where I am, and I'm content with all my accomplishments. There are no regrets. What about you?"

"Oh, I'm never becoming a grandfather."

Surprised, I looked at my detective friend. "Seriously? How can you say that when you have two daughters?"

"Daughters, sons, it doesn't matter. The girls are never gonna be allowed to date."

It was my turn to laugh. "And how do you propose to do that?" I asked. "It's not like you can keep them locked up forever. They're eventually going to go on dates, you know."

"Oh, yeah?" Vance challenged. "Watch me. You've seen *Robin Hood: Men in Tights*, haven't you?"

I knew exactly where he was going with this. For those of you who might not have seen the movie, Maid Marian wears a, umm, iron chastity belt that is, quite literally, under lock and key.

"You won't always be able to dictate their social lives," I told my friend. "Sooner or later, you're going to have to trust that you raised them right."

Vance was silent as he considered. Had I made it through to him? "Agree to disagree. Now, you guys go do your thing. See if there's anything in here the dogs notice. If you find something, well, this place isn't that big. Just let me know."

"You got it," I said, as I nudged the dogs awake. "Grandpa."

"Not funny," Vance scowled.

"Depends on where you're standing," I laughed. "Sherlock. Watson. Come on. Let's check the bedroom, okay?"

The room was just as tiny as I imagined, and just as, well, expected. It was dark and dingy, with dirty clothes flung everywhere. The room was just about taken up by a huge king bed, with a large headboard, twin nightstands, and a matching dresser. Judging from the color of the wood, I'd say it was either black walnut, or else someone wanted to find furniture made of the darkest wood imaginable. But, the problem was, the furniture was too large for the room. There was a narrow walkway around the bed that was literally less than a foot wide. It was so narrow that the drawers couldn't be opened on the nightstands and the dogs had to walk single file. Ever see a corgi walk in reverse? Trust me, it's hysterical.

"Someone sure had his priorities out of whack, didn't they?" I asked the dogs, as I let them sniff around the bed. "Just don't look too hard, would you? You never know what you're going to find in here."

I slid open one of the closet doors and let the dogs poke their heads inside. Sherlock snorted once, shook himself, and then pulled on the leash, eager to leave the room. Watson was right behind him.

"Anything in there?" Vance asked.

"Not a thing, unless you count lack of floor space as an issue. There's barely enough room to walk around the bed in there."

"Yep, I noticed that, too. The bathroom is just over there. See what they think about that, would you?"

"Sure. Sherlock. Watson. Let's go take a look. Okay, we have ... well, we have one final crime scene tech. Sorry, pal. I thought there was no one left in here."

A young guy wearing the uniform of a crime scene technician, wearing gloves, mask, hairnet, and headgear, turned at the sound of my voice. "Don't mind me," a male voice announced, as he finished swabbing the inside of the sink. "I'll get out of your hair, so you can ... hey, are those the detective dogs I've heard so much about?"

I nodded and wrapped the leashes tightly around my hand. Whenever the corgis meet new people, they always tend to go overboard.

"That's Watson, who's sniffing your feet," I reported. "And Sherlock is the tri-color who's trying to determine if you have a pocket full of doggie biscuits, like Detective Samuelson. They're helping us out with this case. Hey, let me ask you something. Did you see the victim? Can you tell me what the cause of death was?"

"I saw him. They took him away about thirty minutes prior to your arrival."

"And? Do they know what killed him?"

The tech nodded. "It wasn't very hard to miss. Blunt force trauma to his head, I'm sorry to say. He never had a chance."

"Murder weapon?" I asked.

"We figure it's something heavy and flat. Maybe a bookend? Or … or a sledgehammer, I suppose? The problem is, it was about the size of a tennis ball. However, there are no bookcases in here, and not much in the way of knick-knacks. Level with me, would you? Our captain says you guys have solved more cases than the rest of your police department. Is that true?"

I looked through the doorway to see if Vance was listening. He wasn't. Instead, he was busy pulling the couch away from the wall, to see if there was anything hiding beneath it.

"No, absolutely not," I said, but I gave a subtle nod of my head at the same time.

A smile formed on the tech's face. "How do they do it?"

"I wish I could tell you," I answered. "Truthfully? I'd like to know, too, only I've yet to figure it out. And it's not just our police. Several other police departments have also tried to solve cases faster than them. None have won, I might add."

The tech finished swabbing the sink and packed his gear. "You don't say. Can I ask who?"

I shrugged. "Oh, it really isn't that important. The New Orleans police department, for one. Oh, and Scotland Yard, for another."

"Scotland Yard? Your dogs solved a case faster than Scotland Yard?"

"They did."

"Would you excuse me for a moment?"

"Sure. Sherlock? Watson? Now's our chance. Is there anything in here you want to see?"

The tech, carrying his tacklebox-looking kit of gear, walked by, pausing only long enough to offer the dogs a few pats on top of their heads. Sherlock watched the investigator for a few moments before turning his attention to the bathtub. He sniffed along the base, while Watson checked out the baseboards under the sink. Finding nothing worth their interest, I was pulled back to the living room, where we saw Vance pushing the couch into place. His eyes met mine and he gave me a querying look. I shook my head.

There just wasn't anything to find. At least, that

was according to the corgis. As for the forensic tech, well, he was pacing back and forth outside, passing the front window every twenty seconds or so. Maybe he was on the phone? He passed for the third time when we heard him say *goodbye* and finish the call. He walked back inside, smiled at the two of us, and then made a play at pulling his arm up and looking at his watch.

"Got your phone handy? You're probably going to be getting a call right about … *now*."

Right on cue, Vance's cell started to ring.

"You might want to get that."

"What have you done?" I asked the tech, as Vance stepped outside to answer his phone.

"The city of Medford has decided to take you up on your challenge."

"I haven't challenged anyone," I argued. Vance paced by the window, much the same way this fellow had done only moments before. "What's going on? Who's he talking to—Captain Nelson?"

"All I know, it was some lady with the last name of Campbell."

I held up my hands in a time-out gesture. "Wait, wait, wait. He's talking to a woman with the last name of Campbell? As in Debra Campbell, PV's mayor? Who did you call?"

The tech waved off my question. "Medford will gladly break your winning streak for you."

"There's gotta be some type of wager involved," I decided, "or that phone call would have been finished long ago. Do you know what's at stake?"

"I don't, I'm sorry to say. I only informed my captain that you and your dogs were here, and the rest, as they say, is history."

Vance suddenly appeared. He leveled a stern look at the forensic tech before waving him toward the door. "Okay, do you mind? I think I need to talk to my friend, here."

The evidence technician glanced at me and nodded. "May the best police department win."

Once we were alone, Vance sighed. "Here we go again."

I squatted next to the dogs. "Hit me with your best. We clearly have another wager happening. Let me guess, we have to solve this murder before our Medford neighbors do?"

"Yes. I don't know who that guy was, but he managed to get a dangerous game started."

My smile vanished. "Dangerous? What's going on? Can we politely refuse?"

"The loser," my detective friend began, "has to select five of their officers and turn them into human billboards."

I stifled a laugh. "Which say *what*?"

"I don't know. Something to the effect of admitting we have an inferior police force."

"That doesn't sound so bad," I decided.

"Oh, it gets worse," Vance said. "The victims, er, losers, have to walk around the downtown area of their respective cities for a full hour, in full view of everybody."

"And I'm guessing Chief Nelson wants to be

certain we pull off the win?" I asked.

"What do you think? Of course, he does. The last thing he wants is to be considered second best."

"Medford is one of our neighbors," I reminded him. "Do we really want to make them look bad? It's one thing to compete against someone in another part of the country, or even a completely different country for that matter, but to take on someone close to us?"

"You're not worried about losing, are you?" Vance teased.

"I just don't want anyone to feel bad," I argued.

"Zack, don't worry about it. This is all done in good fun."

"If we lose, *you* are going to be the one wearing the sign," I vowed.

"And you'll be right there, with me," Vance promised.

"Swell."

"So, what have you got?" Vance eagerly asked. "What have the dogs found so far?"

"Not a thing," I said, shrugging. "They've looked in the bedroom and the bathroom, and thus far, nothing has sparked their interest."

"What about the kitchen?" Vance wanted to know.

"That's next on the list," I promised. "In fact, Sherlock? Watson? Let's take a closer look, okay? Don't worry. This won't take too long. After all, I think the bathroom was bigger than this."

Vance stepped aside as the dogs headed for a kitchen that looked to be no bigger than a standard walk-in closet. There was a two-burner electric range, with a tiny oven that was several years past its recommended cleaning cycle. The small, mid-size fridge holding the science experiments was on the opposite wall, and the sink was on the right.

Disinterested, the dogs sniffed once at the fridge before moving to the sink. As in most homes, there were two cabinets located underneath. I cracked open the first door and was reaching for the second when all hell broke loose.

A big fat, black cockroach jumped out of the cabinet, hit the floor, and took off like a shot. Apparently, I'm okay with bugs startling me, seeing how I didn't utter one choice swear word. I did give a small jerk backward, though. The same couldn't be said for my stoic detective friend. Vance let out a high-pitched scream and executed a leap backward that would have made Spider-Man proud. To tell the truth, I was more spooked by Vance's reaction than the presence of the cockroach.

"Jesus H. Christ! It's a cockroach! Get it! Kill it!"

I looked back at my friend and found him standing on the coffee table. "Hmm. You handled that well."

"Bite me, buddy. Where'd it go? Do your thing. Find it. Kill it. Hurry!"

"It's just a bug," I said, as I gave a gentle tug on the corgis' leashes. "Sherlock? Watson?

Uncle Vance the Brave has delicately requested the immediate destruction of the insectoid intruder. What do you say?"

Both dogs barked excitedly. Sherlock and Watson practically bounded out of the kitchen and lunged straight for the living room, where Vance was hiding.

"Don't shoo it over here!" Vance bellowed. "Get it away!"

We saw a black blur zip toward the couch. If a grown man could've scaled walls, then Vance would've done it. I'm surprised he didn't try to jump on my back.

"What is it with you, anyway?" I asked, growing exasperated. "Get off the kitchen counter. Seriously, how did you even make it all the way there from the coffee table? Whatever. I'm not kidding, get down. Are you trying to break it?"

"You take care of that thing and I'll get down."

Sherlock yipped once. He and Watson were now in front of the couch, with their noses shoved under the cushions and their rear ends wiggling with delight.

"You two don't have to look so damn delighted!" Vance scolded. "Zack, don't you dare let them touch that thing. It practically *thrives* in filth and bacteria."

Watson chose that time to break off the frontal attack and try flanking the roach from the opposite side of the couch. As soon as she thrust her nose into the small opening, she woofed a few times, hoping to flush the prey out. Unfortunately for Vance, it worked all too well.

"It's coming right for me!" Vance bellowed, as the roach scuttled toward the kitchen counter, and then *up* it.

I spotted a plastic cup mixed in with the other dirty dishes in the sink, dumped whatever was in it *out*, and quickly slapped it over the roach before it could make it to the underside of the counter.

"That's my man, Zack! Holy cow! That is my worst nightmare, right there."

"It's just a roach," I reiterated.

"Those don't bother you?" Vance asked, shocked.

"I certainly don't want to keep one as a pet," I explained, "and you're right. They're covered with bacteria. Did you know that's the reason why you're not supposed to squish them? It can spread harmful bacteria all over the … hey, man. Are you okay? You're not going to be sick, are you?"

Vance carefully climbed down from the kitchen counter. "No one has to know about this. And no, I'm not going to be sick. At least, I don't think so. Just get that thing out of here. By the way, I hereby swear to whatever gods exist, if you release that thing on me, then I'll make your life utterly miserable. Do you hear me?"

"Loud and clear," I chuckled. The outside door was already open, so all I had to do was slide a piece of paper under the cup, which there were many scattered here and there, and then flick the roach outside. However, before I did that, I noticed the dogs. They were staring directly at the cup covering the roach. Coincidence? "Let me get my phone out, guys. There we go. I took a picture of the cup. Will that work?"

It did.

Sherlock and Watson dropped their fascination with the cockroach and looked over at Vance. Then, they tilted their heads, as if they couldn't figure out why one of us had been perched on the counter.

"Don't look at me like that," Vance scowled. "I'm already going to get all kinds of crap from *him*. I don't need you two doing it, too."

I took the cup outside and flung its occupant into the parking lot, secretly hoping a bird would dispatch it for us.

"All gone. Better? Do you have a phobia about bugs?"

"Just cockroaches," Vance admitted. "Wish I could explain why. Ugh. I hate them. If ever there was something that deserved to be exterminated, it'd be them."

"Sherlock? Watson? Come on, guys. Let's finish this up. Where there's one of those things, there's bound to be more."

Vance let out a groan. "You just had to say that, didn't you?"

"Sorry, pal. Guys? Is there anything else in here you need to see?"

The dogs looked at me, then up at Vance, who

was just now climbing down from the counter, and then straight at the door, which was still open. Sherlock gave himself a good shaking and then tugged on his leash, eager to leave.

"That works for me," Vance said. "If I never see this place again, I won't shed a tear. Man, I think I'd like to take a shower."

Once we were outside, and we were both ready to climb into our cars, Vance's cell rang.

"Detective Samuelson. What's that? You're who? Oh, okay. Yes, sir, I've been made aware of the wager. Yes, sir, I've been advised to say that we *will* be participating. Oh, yes, I've been told what the consequences are, should we lose. What's that? You want to do what? Actually, I would greatly appreciate that, thank you. Just a moment, let me get my notebook." My friend placed the phone on the hood of his car and tapped the speaker button. "If you don't mind me asking, Captain Ryerson, why are you cooperating with us?"

"Fair play," a gruff voice replied. "In the spirit of full disclosure, since my officers were on scene first, you will have full access to everything they've discovered. If we're to beat you, it will be done fair and square, you got me?"

"Loud and clear, sir. Thank you."

"Let's see how you thank me when you get to parade down Pomme Valley's Main Street with *We lost to Medford* strapped on your chest. Or something just as silly, I haven't decided yet."

"Or *We fought the corgis, and the corgis won* for

yours. Sir."

A silence descended. I eyeballed Vance and gave him a worried frown. Had he taken it too far?

A loud burst of laughter erupted from the phone.

"You're on, Samuelson. Should your team of lap poodles beat my detectives, then that is *exactly* what I'll have their signs say."

Vance stifled a laugh. "We look forward to it, sir."

For the next ten minutes, Captain Ryerson of the Medford Police relayed everything he knew about the murder that had happened in his city. Name of the victim, occupation, known associates, employment history, and so on. I have to admit, I was impressed. Captain Ryerson's department had collected an impressive amount of data. In fact, there was so much information to transfer to Vance's little notebook that his hand cramped, and he quickly took the leashes from me when I offered to take over. When the captain finally finished, he wished Vance luck and terminated the call.

"I have to say I didn't expect that," I said, as I massaged my right hand to restore circulation. "I thought for certain we were on our own."

"That makes two of us. Look at this. My notebook is almost full."

I gave Vance a friendly nudge and reached for the handle of my car door when I felt the leashes go taut. Concerned the corgis might have found the cockroach we disposed of earlier, I glanced back to see what was going on. Both dogs were looking left, in the direction of the dumpster.

"Do you see this?" I asked Vance, as I relocked my Jeep and headed in that direction.

"What is it? What do they see?"

"I'm not sure. But, if so inclined, feel free to ask them."

"Jerk. Alright, guys, what are you ... Zack, do you see that? That brown splotch on the ground. It's in front of the dumpster. Doesn't that look like ...?"

"Ice cream," I said. I held the leashes out and, once Vance had taken them, lifted the lid to the dumpster to peer inside. "There better not be another dead guy in here."

There wasn't. But, a large round empty carton *was* visible, complete with drips of brown goo dribbling down the side of the container. It looked like it was made of Styrofoam, was devoid of markings, and it was empty. Mostly.

"Coincidence?" I asked, as I looked back at my friend. "There's an empty, open ice cream container. There aren't any brand names visible, it's just white, like the kind you'd find at stores that sell food in bulk."

Vance peered over the edge of the dumpster and studied the carton. He patted his pockets as he searched for his phone.

"What, you want a picture of it? I've got my phone right here. I'll take it. There we go. One nasty ice cream container. Why do you think he threw it away?"

"You have no idea if our killer is the one who threw that away," Vance told me.

"Just humor me," I urged. "The dogs are interested in it, so there's that. Answer the question. Why get rid of it?"

Vance scratched his chin. "Wrong flavor?"

I grunted and was about to let the lid drop back in place when I noticed something else, on the other side of the dumpster.

"Check that out. Cookies."

"So?"

"It's just curious, that's all," I decided. "Considering how bad everything else in here looks, and smells, those cookies aren't too bad. What are they, sugar? Peanut butter?"

Vance waved me on. "Have at it. If you want to crawl in there, be my guest."

"Ugh. Forget it. I'll take a pic of it, just in case. Oh, wait a moment. It shows in my last shot, of the ice cream container. We're done here. Guys? Shall we go?"

Sherlock and Watson each snorted at the same time and headed the opposite direction, which was where our vehicles were parked. But, before I could think about returning home, a notion occurred. I pointed at Matthew's apartment.

"I want to go back inside."

"What in the world for?" Vance wanted to know.

"I want to check a hunch."

"Be my guest. I'll wait right here, thank you very much."

"Baby. Take the leashes. I'll be right back."

Once inside, I headed straight for the kitchen. Bachelor or married, there was always a cabinet that had a few spices in it. I wanted to see if they had been disturbed.

I selected the cabinet closest to the stove and cautiously opened the door. The last thing I wanted was to have a cockroach surprise me by jumping out at me, or running across my hand. I didn't want to give Vance that satisfaction. So, with the cabinet door partially open, and a comforting lack of escaping insects, I inspected the interior. Yes, this was the spice cabinet. I could smell the pepper, and something I'm pretty sure was cinnamon. However, there weren't any spices to be found!

"What the heck is going on 'round here?" I asked out loud, picturing myself using a Donald Duck voice.

"What did you find?" Vance asked, once I was back outside.

"The spices," I said.

"What about them?" Vance wanted to know.

"Did you see the dust? Someone opened that cabinet and, from the circular marks in the dust, moved a few things around, as though they were searching for something."

Vance consulted his notes. "That little fact

definitely wasn't in the Medford PD's report. Why would someone take the spices?"

"And *that* would be the million-dollar question. I have no idea."

"What made you check to see if they were there?" Vance wanted to know. "How does an empty ice cream carton and a discarded box of cookies inspire you to look for spices?"

"I'm starting to wonder if our perp might be after an ingredient in the ice cream. I saw the cookies, and I thought that, since they were there, our fugitive took them for a closer look. When he discovered they weren't what he wanted, he threw away both of them."

"Nice theory," Vance decided, "but we don't know if that's what he was after. Yet. Guys, is there anything else you'd like to sniff out?"

When there were no further objections from the dogs, we parted ways, seeing how we drove here in separate cars. I immediately called Jillian, to let her know what I found.

"More ice cream?" Jillian asked. "And spices? I don't see how the two are connected."

"I had a theory, but Vance shot it down," I admitted. "I'm still clueless. Hey, I thought up a new name for you."

"Go ahead."

"Naboo."

"Naboo? No. You already submitted a Star Wars name."

"Fine."

"I have one, if you'd like to hear it."

"Please. Go ahead."

"*Corazón.*"

"Isn't that Spanish for heart?"

"It is. You've been studying!"

"If I can't choose two Star Wars names, then you can't choose two words meaning the same thing."

"I'm sorry? I haven't submitted *corazón* yet."

"But, you *have* suggested *du coeur*, remember?"

My darling wife fell silent, and I'm sure she was blushing. "I didn't think you understood the reference."

"And I didn't. That is, not until I just looked it up. Imagine my surprise when I learned it was two words, not one like I thought, and it was French, which translated to *from the heart*. So, that's two hearts you've suggested." I made a noise like a game show buzzer. "You're disqualified."

Jillian's laugh was genuine and full of mirth. "I'm beginning to think we'll never agree on a name."

"I'll keep trying various sci-fi suggestions," I promised. "I'll find one yet that you'll love."

"We'll see about that, my dear."

FOUR

Y ou must be proud of yourself. Look at this. Can you believe this is really happening? I'm so proud of everyone!"

A day had passed. The PV Charityfest, as the locals were now calling it, was in full swing. Honestly, I had no idea how my little idea had grown so big in such a short amount of time. In less than two days' time, it had grown so much in popularity that our event was featured on both our local radio stations *and* Medford's newspaper, the *Mail Tribune*. Then again, I couldn't be prouder of my fellow PV citizens. We received so many donations, and accepted carload after carload from local businesses, that we ran out of space. Both sides of Main were lined with folding tables, card tables, and anything else that could offer some counter space. Coats, jackets, shirts, pants, bags of socks, and even boots and shoes, had been stacked at various drop-off points. I glanced farther down the street and saw people sorting and stacking blankets, sleeping bags, some tents, and a myriad of other camping supplies.

On the flip side of the street, was an equal

number of tables, but these ones were loaded with food. Non-perishables took up the most space, but there was also a large amount of donated food. Casa de Joe's dropped off pans of individually wrapped burritos, tamales, and enchiladas. Sara's Pizza Parlor brought at least thirty mini personal pizzas. Wired Café brought bottles of water. Several other restaurants brought a selection of their favorites, all individually wrapped. And Jillian? Well, the two of us must've purchased nearly a thousand dollars' worth of gift cards apiece. We divided them up among everyone who was helping us give these items away, so that the people who showed up to claim an item (or two) would be able to get something to eat also.

Overseeing the food tables near Cookbook Nook was Sydney and her huge group of friends. They had been tasked with finding the best method to get the food into as many hands as possible. As it turns out, the simplest was the easiest. They created a buffet line that was nearly two-hundred feet long.

As for me, I'll be honest. I wasn't in the greatest of moods, but that was only because I wasted a solid chunk of my day chasing down leads from the Matthew Hansen murder, and not a single one of them had panned out. I think I even had the Medford police feeling sorry for me, seeing how I've been hard at work trying to link the two brothers' murders, and didn't have diddly squat to show for it. Also, someone kept texting me various pictures of people wearing visual billboards, no doubt as an attempt to rattle me.

It was working.

My spiral downward began the moment I arrived home yesterday, after exploring Matthew's tiny apartment. Three solid hours of online research netted me a small handful of possibilities. I woke up bright and early this morning, figuring I was going to bust this case wide open. After all, I found traces of a former friend of the family who had a criminal record. Turns out this friend had less than scrupulous business principles, and talked the two brothers into investing some capital into a risky business venture. Long story short, the money was lost, the business folded, and the three investors went their separate ways.

In this case, I knew Russell Wilcox was not responsible for either of the murders, because he had been involved with an unrelated crime, and was therefore a resident of the state and quite unable to go anywhere. There was no way he could have had anything to do with the murders, unless he had somehow managed to convince the Columbia River Correctional Institution to release him several years earlier than planned. So, strike one.

Then, I learned Matthew had taken a high-interest loan several years ago at one of those check-cashing institutions, where it takes *years* to pay off the debt. However, when I checked with the company, I learned that Matthew had done just that: he repaid the loan, making the rest of his account officially clear. That made strike two.

Finally, I learned Matthew had been in a relationship with a woman while he had been married. Was this the reason why he and his wife separated? Well, I was able to track down the woman online and give her a call. I had no idea how she'd react to the news of Matthew's death. Sadness? Anger? Despair?

Try none of the above.

What was she? Indifferent. She claimed the two of them grew apart, and she therefore dumped him. I sensed there was more to that story. However you look at it, it wasn't the reaction I was expecting.

"That's too bad," she said, after I first broke the news Barbie Rax's former lover was dead. I kid you not, that's her name. It was on her driver's license. "I really liked him. He just couldn't get his priorities straight. Oh, well. I ain't gonna lose any sleep over it, am I?"

I could tell she meant it. Alive or dead, Matthew didn't matter any longer. She later claimed it was because she had moved on, but she confided to me that it was because Matthew was broke. He had made some bad business decisions, and in turn, it left him destitute, which was something Barbie didn't want to live with.

Forty miles and five hours later, I was back in PV, to help set up tables and supplies for the last-minute charity event I had seemingly pulled out of thin air. Much to my delight, it looked like everyone who was anyone in town had volunteered in some fashion, whether it was to donate much needed items, or simply offer their services.

Stacks of coats and blankets were displayed in front of Cookbook Nook. One of the nearby clothing stores offered the use of two of their hanging display racks. Two tables of mittens and scarves were in front of Hannah's store. She and her son, Colin, were already seated in front of Apple Blossom, anxiously waiting to see if anyone would take us up on our offer.

I sensed movement in my peripheral vision. I looked up in time to see a figure dart between the buildings. Feeling movement from the leashes, I noticed Sherlock and Watson were staring at the same spot. Someone was there. Perhaps it was a poor, hapless soul looking for something warmer to wear? Or, maybe, looking to grab a bite to eat?

"Come on, guys. Let's grab a seat."

"What's the matter?" Jillian asked.

"I think we might have our first recipient, only I think he's scared of us. So, we're going to have a seat and see if we can look a little less intimidating."

"Good idea. I'll join you."

However, fifteen minutes later, we were still waiting, but then again, so was our shadow.

"I don't know what the hold-up is," I admitted. "It's not like we're charging anyone for this stuff.

Why wouldn't he help himself?"

Sherlock rose from the ground, stretched his back, and then looked at Cookbook Nook's front entry. Then, he looked back at me and turned to look inside the store.

"You want us to go in? Why would … oh. Hmm. You might be on to something."

"What does he want?" my wife asked.

"I think he wants to go inside. He may be right. I don't think this guy is going to put in an appearance until the tables have been left unattended. So, let's step inside and see if that lures him out."

It did. Less than two minutes later, a scrawny fellow wearing tattered cargo pants, a thin t-shirt, and a dirty blue jacket appeared. He looked at the stacks of folded sweatshirts and blankets before turning to a rack of old and new coats hung on one of the two display racks. Then, sensing he was being watched, he made eye contact with me.

The individual was anywhere from his mid-twenties all the way up to forties. I couldn't tell. What I could determine was the fact he was male, needed a shave, and (I was willing to bet all the tea in China) could use a shower. I also spotted a dirty white strip of cloth wrapped around his left hand. A wound?

I held out a hand, indicating he could help himself. He nodded once, snatched the top blanket on the stack, and scurried off.

"Medicine," I said, more to myself. "We didn't

consider offering medicines."

"Medicine?" a voice repeated. Turning, I saw my best friend from high school, accompanied by his family. "Hey, bro. How's it hangin', Zack? What did you say about medicine?"

It was Harry Watt and his wife, Julie. He and I attended the same high school in Arizona, and somehow, the two of us ended up in this same small Oregon town. Like me, he was married, but unlike me, he had kids, who I didn't see with him today.

"You managed to talk Drew into watching his siblings?" I asked, impressed. "How much did that cost you?"

"Use of my van for the weekend," Harry said, shrugging. "It was a small price to pay."

Harry often used his van to pick up supplies for his veterinarian business. I pointed at the tables.

"We should have brought some type of medicine kits for these people. That last guy looked as though he had some type of rudimentary bandage wrapped around his hand."

"Hi, Zack," Julie said, as she gave Jillian a hug. "How have you been? Thank you for setting this up. The people could use the help. Did I hear you say you need some medicine? I'm guessing to give away? We're on it. Harrison? Run over to Gary's Grocery, would you? Buy some boxes of bandages, maybe some alcohol wipes."

"Toothbrushes and toothpaste," Jillian added.

"Vitamins," I said.

"If I'm gonna buy anything, I'll buy them some deodorant," Harry said. "Man alive, I don't see anyone here, but the smell is so bad I can almost *see* where they were standing."

Julie smacked her husband on the arm. Hard. "Harrison, you have no idea what these people have gone through. What they're *currently* going through. Don't judge until you've walked a mile in their shoes."

"Yeah, yeah. That smarts. Great aim, Jules. I'll be right back."

"How are the twins doing, Julie?" Jillian wanted to know. "Are they walking yet?"

"Oh, heavens no. But, they're close. They've just learned to crawl, so I have my hands full all the time. I kid you not. Shawn will take off in one direction, and Andi picks the opposite. I can't keep up with them!"

"Have you been losing weight?" Jillian asked, giving her an appraising stare. "Good for you."

"I'd like to take credit, but I can't. You try keeping two crawling kids out of trouble day in and day out. It's like herding chickens. I let Harrison put a pedometer on me one day, after inferring that taking care of the kids was a piece of cake."

"And how many thousands of steps did you end up taking?" I asked.

"It was over twenty. It was the perfect day to make my point. Shawn and Andi had just started crawling. I hit ten miles that day."

I whistled. Whoever said raising a child wasn't difficult clearly has never raised one.

"How goes the case?" Julie asked.

I shrugged. "Not well. I haven't found anything that pans out. Yet. But, I have faith in the dogs. We'll find out who murdered Jillian's thief *and* why someone would want to steal the ice cream."

My friend's wife looked up. "Ice cream? You think the theft of the ice cream has something to do with the murder?"

Julie also happens to work at the PV police department. She wasn't an officer, but someone who was skilled enough to fill in where needed. Usually, she could be found on the other end of the call when someone picked up the phone to dial for help.

"Murders," I corrected. "Plural. Our victim had a brother in Medford, who just so happened to also be a recent victim of homicide. I think everyone knows the two murders are related, only there's no evidence to suggest otherwise."

"I hadn't heard about the brother," Julie confessed. "And for the record, I do know about the wager. I'd love to see Medford cops parade down Riverside Avenue wearing signs saying they were beaten by us. Tell me what I can do to help."

"Keep me from having to put on one of those billboards and march down Main," I pleaded.

"You're not a police officer," Julie pointed out. "I'd think you'd be in the clear."

"Vance has told him that, should we lose, he's

definitely going to be selected to wear a sign. If he has to, then …"

"… you'll have to," Julie finished, giggling. "I get it."

"Since when have Medford and PV had such a rivalry going on between them?" I asked.

"Since you and the dogs became police consultants," Julie answered, without missing a beat.

"Ah. You're saying this is my fault?"

"I think she's saying it's Sherlock and Watson's fault," Jillian corrected. "The corgis are just too good at finding clues."

"And we already know we suck at figuring them out," I reminded everyone.

"I'll do what I can to help," Julie promised. "We won't let Medford win. Just tell me what I can do."

"I think Vance has it covered," I told her. "I mean, I guess if you hear something about the case, then shoot me a text, okay?"

"You got it. Look, we have a few other takers."

Three men had appeared. We could tell they knew each other by the way they kept together. With every step they took through the many tables of offerings, they became bolder. After a few minutes, you'd think they were taking a leisurely stroll through a department store. One man selected a blanket, then tried on a few coats, and finally, selected a pair of gloves. The next person did the exact same thing, only he must've gone through half a dozen coats before finding one he liked. I should also point out that Hannah was quietly following behind the shoppers and re-folding the blankets to return to the tables, or rehanging the jackets that were not selected.

Thirty minutes later, Harry was back, carrying at least five grocery bags full of supplies. Somehow, a new table was produced. We managed to squeeze it in next to several others on our side of the street. Together, Harry, Julie, Jillian, and I hurriedly set out mini first aid kits, bandages, antiseptic wipes, and a variety of other medical supplies. However, the medical table, as I called it, was barely visited. I think one box of bandages went out the entire time. Wish I could say why.

After the first hour, word must have gone out in the homeless community. We were swamped. People were practically appearing out of thin air. One moment, there were only two people perusing the offerings, one on either side of the street. The next, it was standing room only. Warm attire was handed out, camping gear was given away, and everyone who asked was given restaurant gift cards, ensuring no one went hungry for the next couple of days.

I knew PV had a homeless problem, but I had no idea it was so bad. We handed out items to everyone, from teenagers to senior citizens. I was beginning to suspect that, somehow, people from Medford and its surrounding communities had also found their way here. Again, don't ask me how.

The only problem that arose was centered around the food tables. Talk about the biggest clusterf—my bad. I shouldn't swear. I know our homeless neighbors were hungry. As a result, everyone tried to snatch as much as they could, as quickly as they could. Sydney came up with the winning idea. The teenager quickly sprinted across the street and ducked into Cookbook Nook. Moments later, with her arms full of plastic purchase bags, she and a few others started filling the bags with various food items, and including a bottle of water. Others noticed how well that seemed to be working, so while several kids positioned themselves to hand out bags, others went down the food line to keep filling more.

"You need to give that kid a raise," I said, as Jillian and I watched Cookbook Nook's manager effortlessly keep the lines moving. "Maybe she worked for Disneyland in another life?"

Jillian swatted my arm. "She thinks well on her feet, don't you think? And you're right. She deserves a raise."

After the third hour, the crowds began to diminish. There was a very sizeable dent in the supplies of clothing. More than two-thirds of the food was gone, which wasn't surprising, and the food cards were completely gone. I felt a presence on my right. Harry had appeared, and was now sitting on a chair, drinking a bottle of water.

"I need a beer."

"No, you don't. I know you've given it up, pal."

Harry's mouth opened, presumably to protest, or throw his wife under the bus.

"No, you don't. You can't blame Julie for anything. I know you're doing this for her. And look at the results! You've lost, what, at least twenty pounds?"

"Thirty-one, bro. Thirty-one. Giving up beer had to be the hardest thing I've ever done. It ranks right up there with trying to keep two toddlers in the same damn room. Let me ask you something."

"Fire away."

"Haven't you ever wondered about Sherlock?"

Curious, I looked over at my friend. Sherlock, hearing his name, did the same. He even tilted his head at Harry, as though he knew his name had been spoken, yet no one was talking to him.

"What about him?" I asked.

"Haven't you ever wondered how he does what he does?"

"You're talking about solving crimes? Of course I have. I've come to terms with never knowing. Why do you ask?"

"Just makes me wonder what I would have done had I known how smart that little dude is."

"Are you telling me that, had you known Sherlock could find clues and solve crimes, you wouldn't have put him up for adoption?"

"Well, yeah. I guess. Maybe? Look at the facts, bro. He's solved every case you guys have worked. They're more famous than either you or I will ever be."

"And does that bother you?" I asked.

"It doesn't bother you?" Harry countered.

"Not at all. Why should it? I'm not trying to compete with my dogs. Let's face it. They're more popular than me, more adorable than me, and better liked than me. I'm fine with all of it. Let's just say, for the sake of argument, that you knew Sherlock was smart. What would you have done with him?"

"I most definitely wouldn't have adopted him out," Harry admitted.

"Would you have tried to sell him?" I asked, growing irritated.

"Hell no, man. I would have kept him."

A young guy approached and eyed my table of blankets. He grabbed two, then his eyes sought my permission. I nodded, and he vanished as quickly as he had appeared.

"What can you tell me about him?" I suddenly asked.

"Huh? Who, Sherlock? You're his owner. You know more than me."

"In most areas, yeah. But what about his breeder? Do you know anything about him?"

"Oh. Hmm. It was a *her*, if memory serves. She was from Washington State. Tacoma, I believe. Anyway, she's no longer in the business of raising corgis."

"And how would you happen to know that so quickly?" I asked.

Harry grinned and shrugged. "I dunno, man.

I guess I might've, well, looked her up. Er, a few times, anyway."

"You were looking to see about getting another corgi from her, weren't you?" I accused.

"Hey, you never know until you try," Harry argued. "It worked with one of her dogs. I thought there might be a chance it'd work with another, even if she didn't work with the breed anymore. But, no such luck. She's no longer a registered breeder. I can't find hide nor hair of her, bro."

"When did you start searching for Sherlock's breeder?" I asked.

"When Sherlock and Watson's fame was growin' by leaps and bounds. For cryin' out loud, because of them, you met the Queen of England!"

"That's true. That's all on them, and not on me. It does make me wonder, though."

"What?" Harry asked. "It makes you wonder *what*?"

"Whether the breeder disappeared because she changed her name."

"I don't think she'd be allowed to join the Witness Relocation Program just because one of her dogs became famous," Harry pointed out, adding a healthy dose of sarcasm.

"No, you knucklehead. I'm talking about her kennel name. Most breeders have a very specific name for their kennel. Maybe she changed the name?"

"How would I find out?" Harry asked, growing interested.

I shrugged. "Contact the AKC? If Sherlock's breeder is, in fact, still doing business as a reputable dog breeder, she should be listed."

"Right on, man! I'll look into it! Thanks!"

"Uh, sure. If you're happy, I'm happy. What about his history? Sherlock's. Back when I adopted him, you told me he had been returned to your clinic for some incompatibility issue. So, I'm asking you what's his story? Do you remember?"

"Let me think, man. Sherlock. No, I'm not talking about you, boy. I'm trying to remember something. Oh. Hey, I think I got it. Sherlock was adopted by a retired doctor here, in town. There was something about a messy divorce, and the dude was lonely, so he wanted to adopt a dog. Sherlock had been here for over a month. His first owner had passed away, if memory serves. The doc took Sherlock home, and I thought that'd be the last of it."

"What happened?" I wanted to know.

"Well, I guess the good doctor was lonelier than I had thought. A few months later, when Sherlock was due for his vaccines, the doc showed up at my clinic with a new missus on his arm. She was easily twenty years younger than him and was only interested in one thing."

"His money," I guessed.

"You got it, bro. Sherlock and the new wife butted heads almost immediately. She complained, saying Sherlock was disobedient, aggressive, and nippy."

"And his owner believed her?"

"Well, let's put it this way. The doc knew he was being used, and he didn't care one bit about what anyone else thought. After all, he thrived on the attention he was getting. What do you expect when you show up at parties with a woman who could be used as a flotation device?"

I came awful close to snotting my soda.

"Gotcha. Knowing Sherlock as well as I do, I'm sure she got more than her fair share of corgi stink-eye."

"The more I talk about this, the more I remember," Harry said, grinning. "The wife—not only did Sherlock not care for her or listen to her, but he kept giving her disapproving looks."

"He does that to me from time to time. Out of curiosity, are Sherlock's former owners still living in town? Makes me wonder what they'd think if they knew the dog they gave up is the same one who has his own fan-run social media channels."

"He does?" Harry asked, surprised. "Since when?"

"Since the footage of him licking the late queen's hands during my wedding went viral. It's all harmless, of course. Did you know those two have a following of nearly twenty-thousand fans?"

"That's insane, bro. Besides, I think you should know that Sherlock's former owner is divorced now. He still lives in town, but I think he's embarrassed about his behavior. He keeps to himself now."

"And the former wife?"

"Became engaged to another doctor, this time in Roseburg, but broke things off when he insisted upon a prenup. She didn't like that."

"How do you know that?" I asked.

"PV is a small town, man. Word gets around. It's all right, though. Things worked out for the best. You saved him."

"He saved me," I insisted.

I spotted Jillian and Julie on the other side of the street, lending a hand to Sydney. She caught my eye and, since the crowds were starting to thin, motioned me over. Standing next to her at the table that held a variety of Mexican food wrapped in foil (that was now mostly gone), was a lady I recognized from several previous encounters. She was probably somewhere between myself and Jillian in age, wore a beige business suit, and white sneakers.

It was Clara Springfield, *nuntius probrosus*. For those of you who don't know the English translation, that's *obnoxious reporter* in Latin. Impressed I speak Latin? Well, don't be. I just know that particular phrase because I once used the term in one of my books, and for some reason, I've never forgotten it.

I approached Jillian and felt my guard going up. Usually, in order to get the Channel 11 reporter to behave, I have to threaten her with all manner of legal actions, but this time around she smiled and nodded at me. I don't know what was more alarming: her presence or her (surprising) manners.

"Mr. Anderson," Clara began, "I hear you're responsible for organizing this charity event. Is that true? Oh, I'm so sorry. Forgive me. Would you be willing to be interviewed for the six o'clock news?"

Polite *and* cordial? And what alternate universe did I just stumble into?

"Umm, sure."

"Wonderful. Is it true you're the one who organized this benefit?"

For the next ten minutes, I explained to the camera how I had decided to organize an event for the homeless. I tried to give all the credit to the fine folk of PV, but Clara wouldn't hear it. She kept thanking me, asked whether or not the corgis were enjoying themselves, and what I was planning on doing with the donations that hadn't found a new home.

I eventually managed to deflect enough of her attention to get her to focus on the circulating people when I noticed something. The homeless people we were helping were mingling with everyone else, and for the first time ever, I don't think anyone was offended. The volunteers had been encouraged to grab a bite to eat, just like their homeless counterparts, and when Sydney and her friends were looking for a place to sit, they were invited to one of the picnic tables that had been set up, which already had a homeless couple enjoying their dinner.

I tapped on the reporter's shoulder and pointed out the scene. "There's something that is worthy of being newsworthy. Everyone sitting together, enjoying a meal. Kids and adults, some homeless, some not."

"That's so beautiful," Clara gushed. She caught sight of her cameraman watching the spectacle, while letting the video camera droop, and thumped him on the arm. "There. Get that. Zoom in. Come on, I want a word with them."

"That was creepy," I said, once she was gone. "Why was she so polite?"

"I told her if she didn't start behaving, then I'd exercise my right to start sitting in on their staff meetings," Jillian said, nonchalantly.

"You *what*? You're telling me you're part owner of their television channel?"

My wife smiled at me and batted her eyes.

"Oh, crap on a cracker. You *are* the owner, aren't you? Why didn't you tell me? You know what? Don't bother answering that. I don't need to know."

"It has its perks. Look at that. Sydney has inspired others to follow her lead. More people are sitting at the tables. Everyone sitting together. You're right. That's something the people need to see. Our homeless problem is out of control. We need to find more ways to help them."

Catching wind that a local news crew was on scene, the people of PV came out in droves.

Friendships were started, stories were shared, and for once, the troubles of the world became obsolete.

"You've done a fine job here today, Mr. Anderson," a new voice announced.

I turned to see a middle-aged woman standing quietly beside me. This was Debra Campbell, Mayor of Pomme Valley. I nodded my head and gave her a sheepish smile.

"I don't know why, or how, it blew up like this, but I'm not going to argue. I think it's nice to see."

"That it is. I think we might just have to start a new tradition. Every year from here on out, we're going to hold the Lentari Cellars PV Benefit."

"Do you have to call it that?" I asked. "Wouldn't something like the PV Charity Event be better?"

"How about we use Chastity Wadsworth?"

This time, I *did* snot my drink. Thankfully, it was water. "No, umm, Lentari Cellars would be fine."

"I thought as much. Good afternoon to you, Mr. Anderson."

"And to you, ma'am," I returned.

I heard a dog whine and realized with a start that it was Sherlock. My head jerked around until I saw him and Watson, lying on their backs, trying to encourage those around them to give them a belly rub. Sighing, I grabbed a bean and cheese burrito and joined my wife and our friends at a group of tables.

"I saw you talking with Mayor Campbell," Jillian

began. "Is everything okay?"

"Yep, as long as you agree naming this event the Lentari Cellars Benefit is okay, and then making this an annual tradition."

Julie nodded. "Ooooo, how nice! You deserve it, Zachary."

"Yeah, well, anyone could've done it. Vance, glad you made it, pal. Tori? Nice to see you guys. Hi, girls."

Vance and Tori's two daughters, Victoria and Tiffany, ages thirteen and eleven, were also present. They started to wave when they noticed Sherlock and Watson and their crowd of admirers. Once more, I was dismissed. The girls hurried over to offer the corgis some scratches, too.

It was a wonderful time. Everyone was happy. The sun hadn't yet set, although I could feel it was starting to cool off. I didn't care. I was having the time of my life with my family and circle of friends. I had actually started to think that maybe I was reading too much into this whole ice cream heist when, in less than twelve hours, I was going to be reminded that not everything was fun and games.

FIVE

T he following morning, which was Saturday, Jillian and I were having breakfast together at Carnation Cottage, one of PV's dozen or so historic houses — and Jillian's personal home— and planning our day when I received a brutal reminder that I was still working a case.

"Hey Vance, what's up? Hey, did you hear that … what's that? You *what*? Oh, man. Yeah, I know where that's at. I'll get the dogs and head over."

"What is it?" Jillian asked, growing worried.

"There's been a second burglary. Like before, this happened at an ice cream shop."

"Huh. What are the odds of that being just a coincidence?"

"Not likely. I'm sorry. I was hoping to spend the weekend doing some furniture shopping with you. I just realized Myst is going to need a few things, and seeing how I …"

"Hold up," my wife interrupted. "Myst? As in that video game? No. What do you think about Valhalla?"

"Which suggests we're Vikings," I chuckled, "or Norsemen. Oh, let's not forget the part about being dead, too."

Jillian laughed and swatted my arm. "Fine."

"We're heading out, my dear. I'll call you when I know what's going on."

"Please do, Zachary. And see if you can come up with something better than Myst."

"Only if you come up with something that doesn't have anything to do with death."

"You're on."

Thirty minutes later, I pulled in beside Vance's sedan. We were at a small shopping complex just off of Crater Lake Highway in Eagle Point, which is a small suburb north of Medford.

"My in-laws tell me there's a great golf course not too far from here," I began, "but then again, I'm not a golfer, so I'll take their word for it. I usually don't come this far north."

"Tori and I like it here," Vance told me, as he popped open the trunk of his car and reached for a large tacklebox-looking thing. He extricated a pair of latex gloves and pulled them on. Then he pulled out a second pair and tossed them to me. "Eagle Point is about three times the size of PV, and they have something we definitely don't have."

"What's that?" I wanted to know.

"A celebrity pot farm."

"I already know there are a number of dispensaries around here," I began, "but …"

"Not like this. This guy has been in a number of movies, but lately, he puts most of his time into his farm, where he has developed a number of different strains. Maybe it's for different problems? I'm thankful I can say I don't know a flippin' thing about marijuana."

"Who's the celebrity?" I asked.

"Jim Belushi."

"No kidding. He lives here? I'm surprised I didn't know that."

"It's not surprising, pal," Vance told me. "You have as much to do with weed as I do, so I'm rather glad you didn't know."

"Jim Belushi lives in the area. How cool! I've always wanted to make friends with a celebrity. Anyway, the farthest I've ever come is not far from here. There's a restaurant that's only open for breakfast and lunch, but I tell you what, their pancakes are to die for."

"Oh? I love going out for breakfast. What's the name of the place?"

"Breakin' & Shakin'," I answered. "The cinnamon pancakes are worth the trip."

"That sounds like it'd be right up Tori's alley. I know where we're going next week."

"I don't think I've ever stopped in this complex before. There's a grocery store over there. Check out the sign. It says that it's employee-owned. That's worth the patronage right there."

"I've been in there," Vance told me. "Great store. Has a full grocery store, with a deli serving made-to-order sandwiches, and even has fishing tackle. Anyway, it looks like we're heading over there. See the florist? We're right next to it. It sucks to see such a little mom and pop shop get hit like this."

"Why did they?" I wondered aloud. "I know there are a number of larger ice cream shops scattered throughout the area. Why target this one? For that matter, why go after Jillian's?"

Vance pointed at my dogs. "And that's why *they're* here. Come on. Let's go check it out."

The store was a mess. Tables and chairs were upended. Napkins had been yanked out of their dispensers and scattered everywhere. Broken pieces of plastic spoons crunched noisily underfoot as we entered the store. However, we didn't make it far. A full-blown argument was underway, and it looked like it involved the police and the owners of the store.

"Go ahead. Try and stop me. I have rights."

"Mr. Gasbardi, as I've already explained to you," one of the officers said, in an incredibly patient tone, "should you threaten violence, or make any insinuations about pulling out a gun, legal or not, then we're going to have problems. You already have enough on your plate. Let us do our job and deal with the person who did this, okay?"

The man raising his voice was about the same age as me, was wearing corduroy brown pants and a white business shirt. He was short, almost completely bald, with the exception of having fluffy tufts of brown hair just above his ears, and had to have the hairiest arms I've ever seen on a human being. Seriously, it made me wonder whether there was a sasquatch somewhere in the guy's family tree.

"What are they doing here?" Mr. Gasbardi demanded. "And they brought dogs? No! No dogs allowed in here!"

The officer turned to regard us. His mouth opened, readying a response, when he noticed Vance and a grin split his face. "Samuelson! Glad you made it."

"DeVos. Good to see you, pal. What do we got here?"

"Wait a minute," I said, holding up my hands in a time-out. "You're with Eagle Point PD?"

DeVos nodded.

"Our town is smaller than yours. Why'd you call us?"

DeVos motioned us closer. "It's a well-known fact that you guys have a wager going with Medford PD. Anything we can do to help, just name it."

I laughed. "Everyone's out to get Medford, is that it?"

"More like, they're out to get us," DeVos said, under his breath. "Don't get me wrong, they've got some of the finest officers working on the force. However, their captain is one of the most competitive people I've ever met. He doesn't enjoy sharing the limelight."

Vance and I shared a look before my detective friend pulled out his notebook. Coincidentally, I noticed it had been replaced.

"I'll find out what I can here. Zack, take the dogs

and see if they notice anything, okay?"

"You got it. Sherlock? Watson? Let's take a look around."

I felt a tap on my shoulder. Turning, I saw Mr. Gasbardi standing in front of me. "Your dogs? Their names are Sherlock and Watson?"

I offered the shopkeeper a smile. "You've heard of them, haven't you?"

Mr. Gasbardi nodded. "Only because of my wife. I offer my apologies. You have not caught me at my best. Vino Gasbardi."

"Zack Anderson. Don't worry about it. You've got more on your mind to worry about than us. We're here to see if we can figure out what's going on and who would want to do this to you. By chance, do you have any security cameras in here?"

Vino shook his head sadly. "I've never had to worry about it before. This is a good area! Good neighborhood. Never have I had a problem before."

"And now?" I prompted.

"My wife says she has already ordered a system. Comes with four cameras. She says I will be able to watch the store from our house."

"Modern technology. You gotta love it, right?"

"Hmmph. Do you think you can find who did this? If you do, I'll see to it you have free gelato for life."

I perked up. I've long preferred the creamier gelato over standard ice cream. "You're on, pal."

Vino nodded once, patted each of the dogs on the head, and resumed sweeping his floors. I guided the dogs around the store lobby, walking slowly by the tipped-over chairs and the napkin dispensers that, for some reason, had been pried open and were currently empty. A glass display case was on my left. Judging from the chaos inside, I could see that it typically held ice cream cones decorated to look like clowns, ice cream sandwiches, and a selection of cakes and pies. I won't say that every single one of them had been destroyed, but it was pretty darn close. Several caramel-topped pies were now smooshing the decorated cones on the bottom shelf. Cakes had been brutally hacked apart. Smears of frosting, in a wide variety of colors, were everywhere.

"Who pulls apart an ice cream cake?" I asked, as the dogs stopped in front of the display and, together, we surveyed the damage.

Speaking of which, at least it looked as though there was nothing physically wrong with the refrigerated reach-in display case.

"Sure does make you think that whoever did this was in a hurry," Vance decided.

"Or, that's what they want us to think. Any signs of missing ice cream?"

"That was the first thing Mr. Gasbardi checked," Vance reported. "Four tubs are missing: three from the display cases and one from the freezer in the back."

"Dare I ask how the freezer looks?"

"Untouched," Vance said, which surprised me. "Mr. Gasbardi has a large blast chiller, with room for fifty containers of ice cream. Or gelato, I guess. He verified with the Eagle Point cops that someone entered the freezer, searched through their inventory, and took out a single tub. Oddly enough, they didn't touch anything else."

"I'll bet they wanted to, only they ran out of time," I said. "What flavor?"

My friend consulted his notes. "Morning Buzz."

"Morning Buzz?" I repeated, shaking my head. "Who comes up with the flavors for these things?"

"It's coffee-flavored ice cream with a swirl of caramel and has mocha sprinkles."

"I definitely would *not* like it," I decided.

"Still can't stand coffee?" Vance inquired, without looking up from his notebook.

"Can't stand the look, smell, or taste," I confirmed.

Vance looked up, shrugged, and returned to his notes. "It's your loss. What about the dogs? Have Sherlock and Watson found anything yet?"

"Well, they've been taking their sweet time sniffing around the front lobby area, but they haven't stopped at anything yet."

Vance pointed at the narrow corridor to the left of the cake display case. "You can get behind the counters there. Go take a look, will you?"

I glanced over at Vino, who had paused his sweeping. He gave me a nod of permission. I nodded back and gave a gentle tug on the leashes to get the dogs' attention.

"Are you guys ready? Come on. Let's see what's

back there."

Sherlock and Watson took the lead, guiding me to the walkway between the refrigerated case and the long white laminate countertop stretching at least twelve feet long. A series of storage cabinets were directly below, containing tubs of buttercream, racks of food coloring, and bins of various sized bent spatulas. I knew this only because Mr. Gasbardi later explained what was in each cabinet, even though I didn't request it. He must have been watching us explore, and when we hesitated at the countertop, he took it upon himself to answer our (unspoken) questions.

Turning right, we walked along the main display cases, where tubs of ice cream, or gelato, were typically displayed. Customers would then stand on the opposite side and point out which flavors they wanted. As we explored the three cases, I could see, judging by the smears of frosting coating the handles of the glass doors, all of them had been opened. I glanced inside each of the cases, looking for either of the empty spots Vance had mentioned earlier.

"What was there?" I asked, pointing at the first missing tub. I counted the tubs and noticed there weren't enough tubs to fill the spots.

Vance waved Mr. Gasbardi over. "Can you tell us what used to be there? We'd like to know which one is missing."

In case you were wondering why I had to ask which flavor was missing, let me explain. Each tub has its own designated area, with a corresponding tag on the flip side of the display so the customer would know which flavor was which. Well, thanks to the hijinks this thief evidently pulled, practically every tub had been moved out of position. Some were inverted, and others were squished together, making it difficult to determine which ones were in the wrong place.

The shop owner looked inside the case. "Three are missing. Let's see. "Pumpkin Souffle, Banana Orange Surprise, and Harvest Heaven."

Vance had wandered over and I noticed he was scratching out something in his notebook. Correcting the number of missing tubs?

"And these are all gelato?" I asked.

"Yes. No. Wait, let me think. Pumpkin Souffle is, but Banana Orange Surprise isn't. Hmm, Harvest Heaven isn't, either."

Vance drummed his fingers on the counter. "Your shop is called Corner Delights. You're the one who makes all of this?"

Vino Gasbardi smiled broadly and nodded. "Third generation confectioner. My father and his father before him, all confectioners. My shop is the first to be opened in America. I love this country!" Mr. Gasbardi looked back at the mess his store had become and sighed. "Usually. The thing is, I don't remember making those two."

Vance looked up. "Which ones?"

"The pumpkin and the banana-orange. Getting old is for the birds."

Two cars pulled into the parking lot. Both parked at the same time, choosing spaces next to each other.

"Ah, my nephews are here. They will help me with this mess."

Vance nodded. "Glad to hear it. I just need them to hold off doing anything unless we give them permission, all right? The scene has to be processed."

Three young men entered the store. They were probably in their late twenties, or early thirties. All three were lean, had dark complexions, and had jet black hair. Two of the guys took one look at the damage and started swearing in Italian. I had no idea what they were saying.

"Marco! Lorenzo! Tommaso! Enough!"

The three men (brothers?) fell silent, but I could see in their eyes that they were all seething with anger. Two of them looked at me and then, as one, dropped their gazes to the floor.

"Police dogs? Corgis? You cannot be serious!"

Vino cuffed the man who spoke on the back of his head. Based on his previous outburst, I thought for certain we were in for another round of swearing. Instead, the nephew hung his head and fell silent.

"Pay no mind to him," Vino was telling me. "You and your dogs do what you need to do."

"Thanks. We'll head to your back room and … guys? What are you doing? Come on. We need to check back there."

Vino pointed at Sherlock. "Your dogs. They don't want to move, eh?"

I looked back at the corgis and saw both of them staring at the young man who had been reprimanded by his uncle. It's also when I noticed both corgis were sitting. This? This was a corgi clue?

"Him?" I asked Sherlock. "What about him? Why are you staring at him?"

"What is the matter?" Vino wanted to know. "Tommaso, come here. What is with you? Why is the dog staring at you? If you had anything to do with what happened here, then I will personally see to it you get that nose job you've been wanting. *Capisce*?"

"*Sì, capisce*. I don't know why he's looking at me, Uncle. I have nothing in my pockets. No food. What do you want, boy?"

Tommaso squatted low and held out a hand. Sherlock stared at it with what I can only describe as disdain. The tri-colored snout lifted, and those disapproving eyes seemingly looked straight into Tommaso's soul.

"Where were you last night?" Vance suddenly asked, after he looked up from his writing and noticed both dogs staring straight at him.

"Home, of course."

"And your brothers?"

"One is a brother. The other is a cousin. They were with me. We were playing poker."

"You had better not have been playing for

money," Vino warned, from nearby.

"Of course not, Uncle." To Vance, he lowered his voice and gave him a conspiratorial wink. "We were. I won big. You want to know where we were? Now, you do."

Vance nodded, and added the notes. I glanced over at Sherlock and saw that he was still staring at Tommaso.

"Are you holding anything?" I asked the young man. "Are you wearing something you typically don't?"

Tommaso gave me a confused look. "Eh? What you see is what you get: a complete package. The ladies love it!"

I mentally rolled my eyes. Looking back at my dogs once more, I shrugged, pulled out my phone, and when I saw that Tommaso was no longer paying attention to me, quietly took his picture.

Sherlock rose to his feet and shook his collar.

"What was that all about?" Vance wanted to know. "Sherlock was paying attention to him?"

"And stopped the moment I took his picture," I confirmed. "What that means, I don't know. I can only hope we figure it out later when we all review the pictures."

"Roger that. Have you checked out the back yet?"

"We're doing that right now. I'm betting we'll find something."

And I would have lost. Granted, we didn't spend a lot of time looking through Vino's back supply room, but that's because the room wasn't that big. The walk-in freezer took up much of the room, and the rest of the space was occupied by boxes of spoons, cups, wrappers, and everything else an ice cream shop needed in order to stay in business.

As we emerged into the front part of the store, Vance gave me a questioning look. I immediately shook my head no, which earned me a sigh from my friend.

"I'm going to take them outside. Perhaps there's something out there that needs to be investigated?"

Vance nodded and waved me off.

The first thing on my list to check out was the dumpsters. This time, there weren't multiple rows of businesses, which meant I wouldn't find an alley lined with the large trash receptacles. In this case, there was an enormous community dumpster, secured with a large padlock, several hundred feet away. But, I did see a few trash cans scattered here and there. Figuring Vance would want me to be thorough, I walked the dogs past every trash bin I could see.

Still nothing.

"I don't know what else to look at, guys. Sherlock? Watson? Is there anywhere you'd like to go? What about that grocery store over there? Maybe they ..."

Woof.

It was music to my ears. I quickly looked at Sherlock. Both he and Watson had fixated on something, but it certainly wasn't the grocery store. In fact, the corgis were staring across the street at a second mini-shopping area. I could see another long, narrow building housing at least five different businesses. One of them looked like a pizza parlor. Is that what attracted Sherlock's attention? Was he hungry?

"Are you sure?" I asked the inquisitive corgi.

"Awwooowooo!" my little boy insisted.

I took a few steps back from the dogs and tried to triangulate on where they were looking. From what I could tell, they weren't watching the shops on the right, but a second row of businesses that were running perpendicular to the first. The only thing I could tell about this second set was that it included a small barber's shop.

I fired off a text to Vance, letting him know we were walking across the street, and headed off. The dogs were definitely interested in something. Both were pulling like they were oxen, and I was the farmer manning the plow.

"Easy, guys. I don't want you to hurt yourselves. We'll make it over there, you'll see."

There was a break in traffic, which allowed us to hurry across. Once we were in the parking lot, I saw (and smelled) the pizza restaurant. Actually, it was more of a pizza location. I didn't really see anywhere to sit. A couple of young guys were busy making the pizzas while several others would stuff the boxes into bags and hurry out to their cars to make the deliveries.

The dogs wanted nothing to do with it.

We veered to the left, and I thought we were angling for the barber shop, but we didn't make it that far, either. Sitting directly in the middle of the complex was a two stall self-wash car wash. I saw a change machine on the side of the building, and a peculiar looking vending machine, offering rags, cleaners, and air fresheners hanging next to it.

Sherlock and Watson pulled me to the first stall.

"Guys? What do you want with this place? We … oh, pardon me."

The first stall was in use. An older gentleman was busy spraying down a cherry Cadillac sedan, and based on the size, namely that of a small, flat-bottomed barge, it had to be the world's worst gas guzzler. It was big, shiny, and I have to admit, remarkably well preserved.

"Hello, there," the man returned. "I'd stop and say hello, only if I did that, this blasted thing would want me to insert another several dollars' worth of quarters."

I held up a hand. "No worries. Sorry to bother you."

Sherlock and Watson watched the proceedings for a few moments before they each dropped their noses to the ground and started sniffing like crazy.

"What is it?" I asked, curious. "Do you smell something?"

The dogs led me to stall number two. It, too, was occupied. This time, I was looking at a green mid-sized pickup truck. A young kid, who couldn't be more than sixteen or seventeen, and looking an awful lot like a young Jim Carrey, was in the bed of his truck. The tailgate was down, water was streaming out of the bed, and the kid blasted gallon after gallon of high-pressured water at it. That was about the time the smell hit me.

Spices. Something in the air reminded me of thanksgiving, of scented candles, and … pie! Pumpkin pie! Wait. Wasn't that one of the flavors of ice cream from Vino's shop? Pumpkin souffle? Someone wouldn't be stupid enough to steal ice cream, let it melt, and then practically return to the scene of the crime to rinse out the getaway vehicle, would they?

Apparently, that answer was a resounding *yes*.

Sherlock let out a woof, which alerted the kid. His head jerked up and his eyes locked on mine. Shock appeared on his face. A split second later, he jumped over the side of his truck, letting out a curse when he hit the ground. He thrust the water gun he had been holding back into its holder on the side of the stall's wall and leapt into the cab of his truck. The green truck sputtered to life and roared away.

While the kid had been hurrying to replace the high-pressure water gun, and then jump inside his truck, I had calmly activated the camera on my phone and snapped a couple of pictures, making sure I got the kid's face *and* the license plate of the truck. Still chuckling, I dialed Vance.

"Hey, Zack. Listen, we're not …"

"Hang on a second, pal," I interrupted. "Get out your notebook. No, don't argue, just do it. Take this plate down." I relayed the plate numbers to my friend. "I'll send you his picture, too."

"Who is this guy?" Vance demanded.

"Oh, just someone Sherlock and Watson led me to, a kid who was busy cleaning out the bed of his truck. Is this the part where I mention he was rinsing off melted ice cream and that it smelled an awful lot like pumpkin pie?"

"Pumpkin souffle!" Vance breathed. "I'll be damned. Your dogs rock, Zack! I'm calling this in. DeVos is here, too. He's gonna do the same."

It took less than fifteen minutes. Thanks to the small size of the town, the local police department quickly located the 1994 Ford Ranger, still dripping with water, concealed beneath a tarp in the owner's carport. The driver, eighteen-year-old Barry Foster, insisted he was innocent as he was placed in handcuffs. His parents, specifically his mother, offered up what they knew about the stolen ice cream tubs. Apparently, they told their son they didn't have room to store objects that size in their freezer, so Barry had left with three of them. However, there were supposed to be four. That meant one tub was still missing.

The dogs guided me to the household's trash bin, located under the carport, next to the truck. I checked inside and found what was left of Morning Buzz. It was buzzing, all right, but that was because a group of flies had discovered the remnants of the delectable treat and wouldn't leave it alone.

"Is this about that stupid ice cream?" the kid's mother demanded.

She, like her husband, was in her late thirties and were very clearly not dressed to receive visitors. Thin, white tank top, red boxers, and brown leather slippers. That, I'm sorry to say, was the mother. The father had on a black muscle tee, blue plaid pajama bottoms, and mismatched socks.

"Your son is being detained for questioning," Officer DeVos was saying to the parents. Neither looked like they were fully awake, even though it was the middle of the day. "This is in connection with the burglarizing of several businesses, one here in Eagle Point, and the other in Pomme Valley. This is Detective Vance Samuelson, from PV. He'll be escorting your son to Pomme Valley for further questioning. Do you have any questions or comments?"

"This is the part where I remind you my deadbeat son is of legal age," the mother announced, "and as such, he is responsible for his own actions."

"Go to hell," Barry sneered, having overheard his mother as he was shoved into Officer DeVos' squad car.

The father sighed. "Where will he be taken? How much is this gonna cost me?"

While Vance filled in Barry's mother and father,

I approached DeVos, intent on asking a question, but he beat me to it.

"You're wondering why we're willingly turning over a suspect to your department?"

Talk about taking the wind out of your sails. "Well, yeah. This is your bust. We're out of our jurisdiction. Why give him up?"

"Oh, we're not giving him up. My captain has been in contact with your captain. As I mentioned before, he'd love nothing more than to see MPD knocked down a peg or two. So, I've been ordered to cooperate and, this is a direct quote, help our brothers in Pomme Valley."

I held out a hand. "We appreciate it, pal. When we win this wager, and we *will*, make sure you have your camera ready. I'd love to see it go viral online."

"You and me both, Mr. Anderson."

SIX

Sunday afternoon found us out for a leisurely drive. Myself, Jillian, and the two corgis had piled into my second vehicle and, together, we hit the open road. As was always the case whenever I drove this particular car, we got some envious looks. Jillian and I had also made a friendly wager, namely to see how long it'd take to come across someone who would try to buy it from me. She said it'd be the first opportunity someone could talk to us. I said we wouldn't get our first offer until we arrived at our destination.

Have I piqued your curiosity yet? No, I wasn't in my Jeep, nor were we in Jillian's SUV. We had elected to take the Ruxton. I've been told my roadster is in cherry condition, but that's only because it had been lovingly maintained ever since it had been purchased by Dame Hilda Highland, presumably in the 1930s. Originally painted in shades of gray, I had changed the color to a dark forest green, keeping it in theme with the traditional horizontal stripes set in various shades of the base color.

Trust me, this thing is sharp.

The Ruxton had just coasted to a stop at the intersection of Delta Waters and Crater Lake when I heard the revving of a motor. A second car coasted in, taking its place in the left-hand turn lane.

"Hey, buddy!"

I glanced at Jillian before turning to the car next to me. "How's it goin'?"

My usual response when greeting a stranger. It might sound indifferent to some, but for me, it works.

"What kind of car is that?"

"It's a 1930 Ruxton Model C Sedan," I reported.

"You're kidding! It looks like it could've just rolled off the factory floor!"

I knew what was coming. "Thanks. Believe it or not, I'm only the second owner."

"You gotta let me buy it," the man implored.

I took a good look at the guy. He was in his mid-fifties, was wearing designer sunglasses, and was driving a 1979 Corvette Stingray convertible, painted a fire engine red. If anyone had the ability to come up with a suitable offer, I was willing to bet it'd be this guy.

"It's not for sale, but thanks for the offer."

"Aww, come on! Classic cars like those, in such great condition, are impossible to find!"

"Is the light green yet?" I whispered to Jillian. My wife giggled and shook her head. Sighing, I turned back to the Corvette driver. "Don't I know it. I think there were only a hundred of these made, and only a handful are still road worthy."

"I'll trade you," the man offered. "Straight across. My 'Vette for your Ruxton."

"No deal, I'm afraid."

Thankfully, the green arrow appeared, enabling the Corvette to make a left turn.

"Last chance, buddy! Are you sure?"

A horn honked. The line of cars waiting to turn left weren't keen on waiting their turn.

"Sorry, pal. You have yourself a good day."

The red sports car drove off.

"Who won?" Jillian inquired.

"Well, we're out of PV. This is Medford, so I guess it took longer to get our offer. That means you won, my dear."

Jillian clapped her hands. "That means I get to choose where we get lunch. Wonderful!"

"Just don't choose that vegan place," I pleaded.

Jillian gave me one of her million-dollar smiles and sat back in her seat.

Ten minutes later, we arrived at our destination: Sweet Tooth Creamery. This place, as I learned earlier, supposedly has a unique selection of flavors, but only in ice cream. Sadly, they didn't offer any gelato. Jillian, it would seem, preferred ice cream over its much creamier, much tastier cousin, and we were here to see if my darling wife could sway me over to the dark side. Plus, we wanted to see for ourselves what flavors this shop held and see if they were comparable to the flavors of the two businesses which had been robbed.

After all, we were still at a loss as to how the two previous shops tied together. That's what we were doing today, looking for ideas.

"This isn't going to work," I said, as we entered the store. "I don't care *what* flavor combination they can come up with. There's simply no beating the creaminess of gelato. They'll always win, hands-down."

"Don't knock it until you try it," Jillian said, as she waggled a finger in front of me. "I'll make a believer out of you yet."

We stepped up to the counter and were greeted by a girl in her early twenties. She was short, perky, and had her blond hair pulled back into a high ponytail. She looked expectantly at us as we considered our options.

"Are all of these made here?" Jillian asked.

The girl nodded and indicated the large white door at the corner of the room behind her. "Every single one. We make everything from scratch, which includes brownie pieces, caramel sauce, butterscotch, hot fudge, and so on. What? What is it?"

"Don't mind him," Jillian said, smiling. "Zachary loves butterscotch. I think he may be drooling."

"Ha ha," I scoffed, but not before wiping my mouth with the back of my hand. "But, she is right. You make all of your own butterscotch? Might I inquire what you use it in?"

The girl shrugged. "Well, it's in Scotchmallow,

one of our best-sellers. Would you like to try a sample?"

"Based on the name alone, I will say absolutely. What's in it?"

The girl retrieved two spoons, but noticing Jillian shake her head no, returned one to the small bin of plastic utensils.

"It's a light butterscotch flavored ice cream, with a thick ribbon of butterscotch and marshmallow swirled about."

"Oh, now you're talking. Wait. You knew about this flavor, didn't you?" I said, whirling on my wife and giving her a mock glare. I popped the sample into my mouth and sighed with pleasure. "Okay, you're forgiven."

Jillian grinned. "Do I win? Is ice cream better?"

"I certainly haven't found any gelato that tastes like this," I said. "Very well, you win."

My wife gave a delighted laugh and ordered herself something that had about five different flavors of chocolate. I think the name of the ice cream might have actually been *Death By Chocolate*. She gave me a small bite, and let's just say it took care of any and all chocolate cravings for the next two months.

I ordered two small cups of whipped cream for the dogs, and followed Jillian back to the Ruxton. The shopping complex we were in wasn't that big, but sure enough, we had a small crowd of admirers around the car by the time we got back.

"It's one of those old mafia-type cars!" I heard

one teenager exclaim.

"It's an old Cadillac," the kid's father sternly corrected him.

"It's no such thing," a different man exclaimed. "Caddies don't look like that. No, this is a 1937 Wolseley. I'm certain of it. This car? It's British."

The answer sounded so definite, so certain, that heads were nodding.

"It's a Ruxton, and it's American," I clarified, as I reached around a bystander to unlock the door for Jillian. "You're close on the year, though. It's a 1930 Model C." Securing my wife inside, I loaded Sherlock and Watson into the car and crossed to the driver's side. "Take it easy, guys."

"Hey, would you be interested in …"

I wasn't trying to be rude. I only half-heard the request, and the door was already closing. I shook my head at the hopeful car buyer, and we were off.

"Don't make a mess," Jillian warned, as she presented the two small cups of whipped cream to the corgis. "Your daddy doesn't like cleaning whipped cream off of car seats."

"I sure don't," I confirmed. "Well, that's one shop down, out of a long list. I don't know about you, but I didn't spot any reason in there that would prevent our ice cream thief from targeting the store. Personally, I think the flavors are better than the last one that was robbed."

"Cookbook Nook didn't have any gelato," Jillian recalled, as we turned left onto Crater Lake Avenue. "I only offer ice cream. Corner Delights had both ice cream *and* gelato."

"And of the two flavors that were stolen, one of them was a gelato," I recalled.

"I really thought it had something to do with the flavors," Jillian said, frowning.

"And it still very well could," I told my wife. "There's a link here, somewhere. We just have to keep looking."

Jillian turned to the dogs and clapped a hand over her mouth.

"What?" I asked. "Let me guess. They're making a mess?"

Jillian snatched my phone from the cup holder and snapped off a few pictures.

"They have got cream all over their noses. Oh, you poor things. They keep trying to lick it off, but can't quite reach it. Let me get a napkin. There you go. All better?"

"*Woof.*"

"Was that Sherlock?" I asked.

"Yes."

"Is he woofing at something he sees, or is he vocalizing his displeasure at being cleaned up, like a puppy?"

"I'd say the latter. You should have seen their eyes, Zachary. When they realized they were going to be given those cups, they each widened so much that I thought they were going to pass out."

"Psycho eyes," I said, nodding. "I've seen them do that a few times. I think it means they're truly shocked and amazed. Where to now? Is there another shop close to us?"

Jillian consulted her phone. "The next closest is in Central Point."

Part of the Medford metropolitan area, the city of Central Point shared its southern border with Medford. As of the last census, it had roughly seventeen thousand citizens, and was currently home to the Jackson County Fair each July. The shop Jillian had selected was about six miles to the north. Easing the Ruxton into traffic, I smoothly shifted gears as our speed increased.

"Oh, you're getting much better at driving this beast," my wife said, giving me a smile.

"Thank you for that vote of confidence," I scoffed, as we picked up speed and turned onto Crater Lake Highway.

"I will admit, you had me concerned," Jillian said. "How many times did you take the car back to Rupert's in order to remove a dent on the bumper, or have the transmission inspected?"

"Hey, it's not my fault this thing has a crazy numbering scheme for its gears," I protested. "Since when is reverse located where first should be?"

Jillian tapped the dashboard. "Since that's how it was for these old roadsters."

"Yeah, yeah. But, you're right. I do like the car, so it was in my best interest to treat it as nicely as I could. It's the least I could do for Dame Hilda and her old car."

Chantilly Cream was located just off the

highway, next to a home furnishing store, and shared its parking lot with the much bigger store. Therefore, there was much more room to show off a prized car, I'm sorry to say. No, not for me, but for someone who had a gorgeous red '57 Chevy parked off to the side. Directly in front of me, waiting to turn, was a red and white '53 Corvette convertible. Once the light turned, it coasted into the parking lot and parked a few spaces from the Chevy. The crowd willingly divided into two smaller groups, and each admired their respective cars.

"Hoo, boy," I muttered, as I entered the lot and cruised past the crowd of people.

Every single one of them, I might add, stopped what they were doing and watched us drive by. I chose a spot directly in front of the ice cream store and parked. By the time I was holding the door open for Jillian, I could see that the crowd of onlookers—all of them—were headed my way.

Jillian smiled as the first admirer arrived.

"It's a Ruxton! Holy cow! Jerry! Get over here!"

We left the crowd to ooh and aah over the car as we walked inside. Sherlock and Watson ignored the people crowding around the car and kept their eyes on us the entire time.

"Look, Zachary!" Jillian exclaimed, as I joined her at the counter. "They have a cold stone."

I followed my wife's finger and saw what looked like a white slab of marble the size of a standard cutting board. "What about it?"

"Look at all the toppings, the fresh fruit, and so

on! They can mix up flavors as we come up with them. Ooooo, what should I try?"

A clerk appeared from the Staff Only door and smiled at us. "Good afternoon! What can I get for you today?"

"You mix the flavors together on that, don't you?" Jillian asked, as she pointed at the chilled slab of marble.

"I do, indeed. You pick what you want, I mix 'em together, and voila! A custom creation, all for you. So, what'll it be?"

"Are you the owner of this place?" I asked.

The man thrust his hand over the counter. "Tim Pratchet. Nice to meet you. Are you the owner of that sweet ride out there?"

I turned to look at my car and saw that the crowd had nearly doubled in size. I also noted—with great amusement—that the owner of the '57 Chevy was one of them. All of them were circling around the Ruxton as though it was roadkill and they were the vultures.

"Yep, that's mine."

"She's a beauty," Tim said, smiling. "Someday, I hope to get something like that. Now, what can I get for you?"

"Just a little info," I said, "and I'll be ordering a double, in a cup."

Tim reached for the container. "You got it. Info? What do you need to know?"

"Have you ever had any problems in here?" I began. "I'm sure you've heard about the two ice cream stores that were hit, over the last couple of days."

Tim was reaching for a scoop when he hesitated. "You're looking into those robberies?"

Jillian raised a hand. "I own one of the stores. The first, actually, to be vandalized. My husband, Zachary, is a consultant for the PV police department, and we were just trying to figure out a link between the two of them."

Tim placed the metal scoop back into the bin of swirling water. "You have my attention. If there's anything I can do to help, just ask. To answer your question, no, I've never seen anything more troubling than a few obnoxious teenagers. Other than that, the area is quiet."

"Have you ever sold something that you didn't make?" I asked. "Say, you encounter someone who makes an unbelievably tasty flavor of ice cream. Have you ever bought anything like that and sold it here?"

Tim was shaking his head even before I had completed the question. "Not once. If I ever come across something that I like that much, I'll buy a bunch of it and simply recreate it on my own. Then, I'll add my own personal twist to it so that it differs from the original."

"Differs?" Jillian asked.

"Make it better," Tim said.

"Reverse engineering," I said, nodding. "Smart man. Well, that answers that. Now, what are your more popular flavors?"

For the next ten minutes, Tim walked us through his best sellers, and then mixed up a few concoctions I was sure I've never tried before. Fudge marshmallow vanilla bean was one. I wanted to see if I could make something that tasted like an Oreo cookie. While it was very tasty, it didn't taste like America's favorite cookie. My other flavor was something I dubbed the Butterscotch Explosion. Vanilla ice cream swirled with a *ton* of butterscotch topping, and then smothered with hot butterscotch. Jillian was shaking her head as she placed her much more sensible order, which was pretty much a fruit salad with a little bit of ice cream added to the mix.

Mine was better.

Thanking Tim for his time, we exited the store only to be met by a huge throng of people. First in line was the '57 Chevy owner. He was dangling his keys in front of him, as though they were the most precious item he owned. Then again, who knows? They might have been.

"Straight up trade, man," the guy was saying. "Your Ruxton for my Chevy. Right here, right now. Title for title."

"No thanks, pal," I said, as I stepped around him. "My Ruxton isn't for sale."

"I've got a '53 Vette," a second man proclaimed. "Same offer, buddy. Your keys for mine. It's right over there. Whadya say?"

"I will say, again, that my Ruxton isn't for sale."

"Aww, come on!" the first car owner protested.

"Everything has a price! Why, I'll … I'll … throw in fifty-grand! That's on top of my 'Vette. How about now?"

"Forget that," Chevy Dude insisted. "I can double that offer *and* throw in my Chevy's keys at the same time. How 'bout now, buddy?"

I tucked Jillian safely into the passenger's seat, closed the door, and slowly turned around. "You do know how few of these were made, right?"

All chatter came to a stop.

"Yep, of course you do. I'm guessing you probably just Googled that. Well, of those, only nine are still running. I'll bet you learned that, too. This one has been garaged and cared for ever since it was purchased, back in the early 1930's. That means this car is in better shape than either of yours, *and* it's much rarer than anything you can come up with."

A collective groan sounded. I held up my hands. "It's not about money. You can each offer ten times what you just did, and the answer would still be no. Why? Because this car was given to me by my wife. It now has sentimental value to it, and as such, I will not be selling it. Ever. So, don't take this the wrong way, but I'm going to have to decline your more than generous offers. You have yourselves a good day."

With that, I ducked inside, started up the big engine, and guided the roadster back to the highway. Once we were on the road, both Jillian and I broke out laughing.

"Never a dull moment," I said, as I worked through the gears to bring the car up to speed. "Well, we're striking out in the ice cream investigation so far. Hopefully the third time is the charm. What's next? Where are we headed?"

"Well, there's a place a little way up the road, but I don't think we'll find anything out there. Turn around. Let's head back to Medford. There's this place near the airport that looks promising."

"You got it."

Once we had reversed direction, and were headed back to Medford, discussion about one of my favorite treats resumed.

"I'm really at a loss here," I admitted. "All these ice cream shops? What's the link? What prompted someone to target Cookbook Nook and Corner Delights? There's no rhyme or reason to it."

"And the thief was killed," Jillian reminded me, "along with his brother."

"All for what appears to be ice cream. Well, it's official. I'm out of ideas. You? What about you guys? Sherlock? Watson?"

Neither corgi paid any attention to me. They had settled into the Ruxton's roomy second row seats and were dozing.

"Thanks a lot, guys," I mumbled. "So, this last place you want to check out? Is it close?"

"The turn is coming up," Jillian announced. "Turn left here."

"At Delta Waters?"

"Yes. Now, at the very next light, turn left. See

the complex straight ahead of us? There's an ice cream store on the far right. Park here and … oh, my!"

I heard movement behind me. Both dogs were stirring. Then, I heard a growl. What was this? Had something attracted their attention?

The parking lot in front of the ice cream shop had two school buses parked near the back. Judging from the number of screaming middle-schoolers, each bus had been packed to the brim. And what do kids absolutely adore? Ice cream.

The line to the shop was out the door. Kids were jumping up and down with excitement, telling loud jokes, and raising their voices so they could be heard over their friends. I almost had an instant headache.

This is the part where I tell you I had my window partly down, and from what my ears were telling me, I wanted nothing to do with any of it.

"*Woof!*"

"*Oooooo!*" Watson added.

"Holy crap on a cracker," I grumbled. "Are you sure you want to do this? Look at all of them."

"I'll stay in the car," my wife advised. "You go on in and take a look around."

I cast a glance at Jillian, who smiled and batted her eyes at me. "You want to keep me safe, don't you?" she protested.

"You want to keep me out of jail, don't you?" I returned, as I set the parking brake and shifted the roadster into Park.

"Try not to maim too many of them. Their parents will notice."

I laughed as I exited.

There's something to be said about being six feet tall and weighing over two-hundred pounds. And frowning. The kids naturally parted around me, like a school of fish would do should a shark put in an appearance.

I chuckled to myself. Wow. Dark thoughts. Come on, Zack. It's just kids. You can do this.

"I'm sorry to tell you the line is out the door," came a harried response, as I stepped up to the display. It belonged to one of two teenage girls who, from the looks of the exasperation and frustration on their faces, were totally unprepared for this impromptu school visit.

"No worries. I'm just looking around. I wanted to see what kind of ice cream you had here. Looks good so far."

The girl offered me a faint smile. "Thanks."

While she scooped ice cream to fill orders, I slowly made my way past the dozen or so kids that were jostling about in front of me. I had to stifle the urge to stick out a leg and trip one of them up when tempers flared and fits were thrown.

"Do you make all your own ice cream here?" I asked, as the same girl passed by me, on her way to the opposite end of the display. She flipped the glass cover open and scooped out some Rocky Road.

"No. All of our ice cream is trucked in. I'm sorry,

I don't know from where."

"Do you have any local flavors?"

Much to my surprise, the girl nodded. She straightened, closed her display, and then pointed.

"Those two there, on the far right. We just got them in yesterday."

"They don't look like they've been touched," I observed.

"Well, take a look at the names and you tell me," she laughed. "Personally, I wouldn't touch them with a ten-foot pole, but the manager was keen to try out different variations."

Curiosity piqued, I stepped in front of the display and read the name tags and their descriptions. Turning my attention to the first flavor: Oregon crostini. According to the description, this flavor was one hundred percent based on flavors found solely in the great state of Oregon, but then again, based on the description of the flavors, I think it was a poor choice to represent our state. According to the placard, this was a pear-based ice cream with crumbles of blue cheese and toasted bread. Did you catch that? Pear, blue cheese, and toasted bread, in an ice cream. No thank you.

The second? Personally, I thought it was worse, and that was saying something. Garden Delight was an avocado flavored ice cream with dehydrated veggies sprinkled throughout. I could see a couple of nicks on the tub's surface, suggesting a few brave souls had tried it, but I didn't see any scoop marks. Whoever made those two had struck out. Badly.

"Egad," I whispered. "Who in their right mind would want to try that?"

"No one," the teenager laughed, overhearing my comment. She moved to the next child in line and plastered a smile on her face. "Good afternoon! And what would *you* like today?"

Wait. Those could be considered gourmet flavors, couldn't they?

I pulled out my phone and snapped pictures of the description tabs and of the ice cream. Nodding my thanks at the girl, I hurried back to the car, only to see Sherlock and Watson were both on their feet and staring at the kids. In fact, it looked as though Sherlock was moments away from barking.

"I was about ready to text you," Jillian told me, as I took my seat. "How was it in there? Hectic?"

"And then some," I agreed. "Check this out. There are two flavors of ice cream that were pretty much untouched."

"Do they make their own?"

"Nope. And the girl said that those two flavors you're looking at weren't up for sale until yesterday. Could it be the same lady you bought yours from?"

"What horrid flavors," Jillian said, shuddering. "No wonder they're still full."

"Right? But, I have to think that somewhere, somehow, those might appeal to someone. I just don't know who. How long have the dogs been on edge? Ever since I left?"

"Ever since we arrived," Jillian corrected. "There's something about this place that has them spooked. Or else there's something there they want us to see."

"Well, it can't be the ice cream," I decided. "I already took pictures. They would have settled down if I did. Wait. Let me try this. Sherlock? Watson? I took pics of the ice cream in there. See? Here's one, and there's the other. Will that work?"

I was ignored.

"I guess not," Jillian laughed. "Look, they seem to be watching those kids."

Several groups walked by us. Neither corgi paid them any attention. Just then, another group of five wandered by. From the way Sherlock and Watson acted, you'd think they were escaped criminals. Sherlock barked, and Watson howled. Thankfully, the kids were laughing and shouting at each other, and enjoying their ice cream. None of them paid any attention to us.

I pulled out my phone and quickly snapped a few shots of the kids. They were just in the process of stepping up into their bus when I took the pictures. Right on cue, both dogs stopped their barking and fidgeting and settled down. Jillian and I shared a look.

"What just happened here?" my wife wanted to know. "How could those kids be responsible? Or, better yet, how could they be related to this theft?"

"There's gotta be some link we're not seeing.

That shouldn't surprise us. We seldom figure out what they're staring at until much later."

"Backpacks," Jillian murmured. "It has to be something about the backpacks."

"Nearly every kid has on a backpack," I protested. "Look at them. Big ones, little ones, bags with broken straps, and just about every color in the rainbow. Why didn't they care about those first two groups? Why the third?"

"I don't have an answer for that," Jillian said, spreading her hands helplessly. "I'm sorry."

"Hey, don't worry about it. We'll have our get-together, we'll all go over the pics, and I'm willing to bet we won't make one iota of progress. Then, once the case has been solved, it'll become blatantly apparent that we are dumber than a bag of rocks. Did I forget anything?"

Jillian laughed. "That about sums it up. Okay, as long as we're headed home, I have another suggestion for you."

"Let's hear it."

"Étoiles."

"And what is that?" I suspiciously asked.

"Forget what it means. Do you like the name?"

I'm not proud of what I did next. I know full well you're never, *ever* supposed to tinker with your phone while you're driving. Well, I'm sorry to say, that was a thought that never once crossed my mind. That is, until my lovely wife literally swatted the phone out of my hand.

"If you must know, it means *stars*."

"Huh. Stars. Well, that's not too bad. If it didn't sound so much like *toilet* we might have a winner."

"It doesn't sound like toilet at all!"

"And the spelling? I'm sorry, it was the first thing that crossed my mind."

Jillian's face sobered. "Well, there's a thought. What about you? Do you have any suggestions for me?"

"Hmm. I actually thought of one earlier today, but like a numbskull, I didn't jot it down. Oh, wait! I've got it! Florin."

"Florin," Jillian repeated. "As in, one of the fictitious countries in the Princess Bride?"

My face lit up. "Yes! Exactly!"

"Don't you want something unique?"

"Well, yeah, I do. I guess I was trying to come up with something I knew you'd like."

"It's a good name, but it's already associated with a very beloved movie. And book."

My cell phone rang. "Hey, Vance. What's up, pal?"

"Zack! Are you busy? I think DeVos has persuaded that little punk to talk."

"Who?"

"Barry Foster. That smug kid who you found washing his truck out in Eagle Point? I just got the call. He says he's tired of being in jail and is willing to do what it takes to get out. This is it, pal! This is what we need to break the case! I just know it! We're gonna win that bet once and for all!"

SEVEN

Early Monday morning, I was watching Vance question Barry Foster in interview room number two. I should also point out that I was sitting behind the one-way mirror watching the proceedings. Sitting directly to my left was Captain Nelson.

"Let's start from the beginning, Mr. Foster," Vance said, as he casually pulled out his notebook and clicked his pen. "For the record, please state your name, address, and occupation."

"Okay, uh, sure. I'm Barry Foster. I live at my parents' house, which is on Elm Street."

"Elm Street," I snorted.

The captain gave me a questioning look before returning his attention to the interrogation.

"And your occupation?" Vance pressed.

"Unemployed."

Vance sighed and shook his head. "There's a shocker."

"Hey, it isn't easy finding a good job," Barry protested. "Eagle Point, White City, or even Medford. Don't judge me. I'm trying! I send out my resume at least twenty times a week. I've probably hit all businesses in this area at least three times this month alone, and that includes those that are here, in PV."

"How hard are you trying?" Vance asked, as he finally looked up. "Opportunities are everywhere. Every place I go, I see a sign in the window. Everyone is hiring. But, what do you end up doing? Something illegal. Can I assume you're tired of being in jail?"

Barry reluctantly nodded. "This is just a big mix-up. I don't belong here. I didn't do anything wrong!"

Vance leaned forward and rested both elbows on the table. "Convince me. Why should we let you go? You were found in possession of stolen property."

"Stolen? Wh-what?"

"And when you saw you were being followed, you tried to lose us."

"I was scared!" Barry insisted. "You would've done the same thing."

"I never would have stolen ice cream in the first place," Vance argued. "But enough about me. Let's talk about you. Was it your idea to steal the ice cream?"

"No, of course not. I was hired to … hey! Don't try to twist the words around. I didn't steal *anything*!"

"Sure, sure."

"He wanted those tubs."

Vance looked up. I also heard the captain sit

upright in his chair. All three of us were leaning forward, eager to hear what Barry had to say next.

"Who?" Vance inquired. "Who wanted those tubs? What was his name? Who hired you?"

"I never got his name."

"How did he communicate with him?" I whispered, forgetting Captain Nelson was sitting next to me. That's when I felt a nudge and saw the captain point at the microphone in front of me. "How did he communicate with the guy?" I asked again, this time holding down the transmit button so Vance could pick it up in his earpiece.

My detective friend looked up, nodded once, and directed his attention on the kid.

"How'd you talk to him? Was it all through email? Did he call you? Text you?"

"He texted me," Barry said. "If you don't believe me, check my phone! Oh, I don't have it with me anymore. You people took it from me when I was arrested."

Captain Nelson rose to his feet and poked his head out the door. "Get the analysis of the Foster kid's cell phone to room two, would you? Thanks, Jonesy."

"Think he's telling the truth?" I asked, once the captain had returned to his seat.

"It's hard to say. Look at him. He appears distraught, no mistake there. Based on what I've seen, the kid truly thinks he doesn't belong here. He thinks he's innocent."

The phone was pulled from evidence and

presented to Vance a few minutes later. Vance pulled on a pair of gloves and slid the phone out of the large plastic evidence baggie. He tapped the screen a few times before he grunted once and slid the phone over to the kid.

"Look, but don't touch. Is this the message you're talking about?"

Barry leaned forward. His eyes lit up. "Yes! That's the one! See? Didn't I tell you? He wanted those tubs of ice cream, and he wanted me to be the one to do it."

Vance took the phone back and scrolled through the conversation. "Says here he recommended you take the tubs by any means necessary. This isn't helping you, Barry."

"But, I didn't steal them! I bought them!"

My eyes widened. He bought the ice cream? All four tubs?

Vance heard the outburst and tried to contain his skepticism. "You ... *purchased* them? Sorry, kid, that's not what we were told."

"Then you were misinformed! I paid for them using my own money!"

"Aren't those tubs expensive?" I quietly asked, as I turned to the captain in the silent viewing room.

He pointed at the microphone.

"Those tubs couldn't be cheap," I said.

Vance nodded. "You want me to believe you're unemployed and you purchased four full-sized tubs of ice cream? How much did that set you back?"

"Over four-hundred dollars," Barry instantly replied. "But, what did I care? I was just paid ten thousand, all in advance. He didn't necessarily say *how* to get the ice cream, only that he wanted them. So, I offered to pay, and the store sold it to me."

"Some guy offers to pay you ten thousand dollars for some ice cream, and you didn't think that was suspicious?"

"He knew," Barry replied. "Somehow, he knew I needed the money. When you're that desperate, you don't ask too many questions. Besides, even though it cost me a little, it was more than worth it to stay out of trouble."

"And how well is that working for you?" Vance said, raising an eyebrow.

"Well, once I get you to believe me, I'm hoping quite well."

"Mm-hmm." Vance looked over at the mirror and the look on his face said only one thing: *now what?*

"Tell Vance we're going to check with the store," the captain ordered.

"We're checking his story," I told Vance, through the microphone. "Hold tight."

"Do you remember the name of that business?" the captain asked. His cell was in his hands and he was furiously tapping away on the screen.

I thought for a moment. "Ummm, Corner Delights, I think. That was the one with the Italian dude and his three nephews."

Captain Nelson nodded appreciatively and stepped into the hallway. That was when I remembered seeing all kinds of mayhem and destruction in the store. If Barry was innocent, then why trash the store?

I returned to the seat next to the microphone and tapped it twice. Vance promptly looked up. "Ask him something for me. If he's as innocent as he says, and he legally bought that ice cream, then why trash the place?"

My detective friend's eyes widened with surprise. A gleam appeared in his eye as he slowly turned to Barry, who at the moment, was slumped in his chair. The kid caught sight of Vance's expression and immediately became defensive.

"What?"

"You expect me to believe you purchased that ice cream, and then you proceeded to wreck the place? Does that make sense to you?"

"What are you talking about? I didn't wreck anything."

"The store was trashed, Barry," Vance said, allowing his voice to become neutral, which had the intended effect of making Barry fidget in his seat. "Ice cream was trashed, chairs and tables upended, and the dessert case ransacked. Why go to all the trouble of staying legit, only to trash the place later?"

"But ... but, I *didn't*!" Barry exclaimed. His wild, frantic eyes were back. "I bought the ice cream and left! You've gotta believe me!"

The door inside my viewing room opened, admitting the captain. He took one look at the scene before him, with Vance giving Barry an accusatory look, and in return, Barry trembling before him.

"What'd I miss?" the captain wanted to know.

I raised a hand. "This one is my fault. I asked a simple question. If Barry legitimately bought that ice cream …"

"… which he did," Captain Nelson interrupted.

That threw me off. "He did? Whatever. Well, if he did, then why trash the store?"

I am pleased to say that the captain's reaction mirrored Vance's. Captain Nelson got a thoughtful expression on his face before pointing at the mike.

"Better let him know."

"Vance? The captain says he confirmed the kid's story."

Vance turned to the window with shock written all over his face.

"The girl who closed the previous night confirmed it," Captain Nelson said. "The owner spoke with her and she said she remembered a kid paying cash for four full tubs."

"I'll be damned," I muttered. "I wouldn't have called that."

"This happened at the end of the night," the captain added.

I grabbed the mike. "Vance? Captain Nelson says Vino confirmed with the girl who worked the previous night. She remembers a kid buying the ice cream and paying cash for it. From what I was told, this was not that long before closing."

Vance plopped into the chair. "Well, well, Barry. Your story checks out."

"Omigod. You ... you believe me?"

"That you purchased the tubs? Yes. But, I will say that I *don't* believe you when you say you didn't trash the store."

"I had nothing to do with that!" Barry whined. "I'm a good person. I wouldn't do that! You saw my phone, didn't you? The guy wanted me to just steal the ice cream. I couldn't do it, so I used part of my fee to buy the freakin' stuff. I figured it'd be easier."

"If what you say is true," Vance slowly began, "then that means sometime between closing time that night and when the store opened the following morning, someone broke in for the sole purpose of, what? Making a mess?"

"Well, yeah! Obviously!"

"I'm not buying it, Barry," Vance told the fidgeting teen.

"Neither am I," the captain agreed. "But, I will admit that this doesn't make sense. There's something we're missing."

Once again, the captain pointed at the microphone and I relayed what he had just said.

"Give me a second," Vance said. "I'm going to confer with my associates."

"I'm not going anywhere," Barry promised.

"What gives?" Vance asked, as soon as he

JEFFREY POOLE

entered our room. "How is this guy not guilty? They confirmed his story?"

"The owner of the store … er, what was his name, Anderson?"

"Vino Gasbardi."

"Right. Gasbardi is more knowledgeable on these blasted cell phones than I am. He made a three-way call, with me and the girl. She not only remembered him showing up to buy the ice cream but could even describe him. Trust me, the kid didn't steal anything."

"Could it be unrelated?" I asked.

Vance shrugged. The captain shook his head before leveling a gaze at me. "A question better left for your two secret weapons, don't you think?"

"Uh, okay."

"Samuelson? Get back in there. See if you can get a description of the person who hired him. I'm inclined to believe the kid's story. For now, anyway. But, before I cut him loose, I want everything inside his head."

Vance nodded. "You got it."

Once he left, Captain Nelson turned to me. "I've got to run. Keep an eye on them. If anything happens, let me know. You have my number, don't you?"

"Your personal cell number? No, I don't."

The captain pulled his cell and immediately dialed mine. I don't know what was more alarming: the fact he had my cell number memorized or that he wanted me to have his own personal number.

"I'll keep you posted."

"Thanks."

By myself, I took my seat and watched Vance pull out the chair and sit back down.

"What's so important about this ice cream, Barry? Did this person ever say?"

Barry shook his head. "He didn't. I wish I knew. But, I somehow got the impression he didn't want me to ask."

A notion occurred and I reached for the mike. "If he wanted it that bad, why was he cleaning melted ice cream from the bed of his truck?"

Vance nodded, gave me a quick thumbs up, and turned to the kid. "When you were spotted in the car wash, you were seen spraying out ice cream from the bed of your truck. Seems rather dumb for the guy to pay thousands of dollars for ice cream, only to let it melt in the back of your truck."

Barry shook his head. "Trust me, no one was more surprised than I was. After all that, he decided he didn't want it."

"Did Barry buy the wrong flavors?" I asked.

Vance crossed his arms over his chest. "Did you mess up and buy the wrong ones? Bet that made him angry."

"No, I didn't mess up," Barry contradicted. "I checked. *He* checked. Those were the flavors he wanted, no doubt about it."

"Then, why did he change his mind?" Vance asked.

"I have no idea. But, what I can tell you is that he was incredibly ticked off about it."

"Did he have to give back the ten grand?" I asked.

"Ask for a refund?" Vance politely inquired.

"Actually no, he didn't. I offered anyway, though."

"And what did he say?" Vance pressed.

"He didn't say anything else to me. He threw the torn tubs into the back of my truck and told me to beat it."

"Torn?" I repeated, confused.

"Torn?" Vance echoed, at the same time.

"Torn," Barry confirmed. "You should have seen him. Once I presented the tubs, he took a kitchen knife to them. Hacked them to pieces."

That was news to me. I promptly fired off a text to the captain. His response came after just a few seconds.

HE WAS LOOKING FOR SOMETHING

"The captain thinks he was looking for something," I relayed.

"Did you watch him while he did this?" Vance asked.

Barry fidgeted in his seat. "Only a little. I was trying to avoid his attention. I didn't want him turning that knife on me."

"Did he find anything concealed within the tub?" Vance asked.

"Not that he said. But, if he was looking for

something, I don't think he found it."

"What makes you say that, Barry?"

"He was angry. So very angry."

"Now, let's talk about this guy. Go ahead and tell me everything you remember about his appearance."

Barry spread his hands. "He had on a mask, a hoodie sweatshirt, and sunglasses. I couldn't see his face."

Vance sighed. "Of course you were going to say that. What about his build? Tall? Short? Skinny? Heavy? How did he sound? If you had to make a guess about the guy, what would you say?"

Barry was silent for a few moments.

"Mr. Foster?" Vance prompted.

"Older than me. Maybe in his twenties? He also had an accent."

Vance perked up. "An accent? What kind?"

"I don't know, really. It was the way he said certain words. It reminded me of ... I'm sorry, I can't place it."

"Foreign country or something like a Boston accent?" I said, into the mike.

"European?" Vance inquired. "Maybe Boston? Sound like the old mafia movies?"

Barry shrugged. "Yeah, maybe like the gangsters."

"Think, Mr. Foster," Vance implored. "Is there anything else you can tell us? Anything, regardless of its importance, could be helpful."

"If I think of anything, I promise you I will let

you know."

TELL VANCE TO CUT HIM LOOSE. DROP THE CHARGES. BUT, HE'S TO STAY IN TOWN.

I texted the captain back, asking if he was somehow watching, but I didn't get an answer. I repeated the instructions.

After Barry rushed by us, eager to be released, Vance joined me in the viewing room. "Oh. I thought the captain was in here."

"He was, earlier. He left about ten minutes ago. But, I think he was still managing to watch what was going on in there. Is that even possible?"

Vance pointed at a small black box off to the right. "The camera is right there. It's all digital, so with the right access, anyone can tap in from anywhere and watch the proceedings. The mike is old school, though. If you want to talk to me, then you have to be sitting there."

"Gotcha. Well, now what? What's the deal with Corner Delights? Who do you think trashed the place?"

"I don't know. I'm starting to think these two incidents might not be related after all."

"What's next?"

Vance was silent as he considered. "There's something we don't know about this ice cream. Our mystery kid clearly wants it for some reason, so I'm thinking there must have been something concealed inside. Why else would a tub of ice cream get hacked apart?"

"What do you want to do?"

"I think we need to talk to whoever is responsible for making this stuff. We go talk to everyone involved. There's gotta be a link in there, Zack. Maybe the same supplier? Or distributor? Maybe they all have the same freezer? At this point, I'd take anything."

I snapped my fingers. "Then, I say we start with Jillian. Let's find out all we can about where she got hers. Then, we'll check in with the others. Want a lift?"

"Where are the dogs?"

"If I know them, and I do, then I'll say they're out like a light on the couch. I can pick them up later, after we talk to Jillian."

* * *

Cookbook Nook's front door was wide open. It wasn't too surprising, since we were having an unusually warm day and Jillian was taking full advantage of it. I spotted a few customers perusing the racks of cookbooks, and a few more going through several aisles of kitchen gadgets, but I didn't see my wife. I *did* spot Sydney near one of the book racks, with a stack of books tucked under an arm. She saw me approaching and gave me a tiny wave.

"Mr. Anderson! It's nice to see you! Are you looking for Mrs. Anderson?"

"I am. Is she here?"

Sydney pointed straight up. "Last I saw her, she

was sitting at one of the tables in the café."

"Thanks, Sydney, we'll head up. By the way, you and your friends did a fantastic job in here. You would never know someone had a field day in here just a few days ago. I really appreciate you helping Jillian."

"It's my pleasure, Mr. Anderson. I think you'll find that there isn't much I won't do for her."

"Glad to hear it, Sydney."

"Let me know if you need anything else, Mr. Anderson."

"You got it. Vance? Follow me."

"Her staff appears to be very loyal," my detective friend observed, as we climbed the stairs to the second floor.

"She has a way with people, that's for sure."

"Zachary!" Jillian exclaimed, as we came into view. She rose to her feet. "Such a pleasant surprise! Hello, Vance! Will you two join me?"

"That's the plan, my dear," I told my wife. "Vance and I have a couple of questions for you about the ice cream you had for sale."

"And was ripped off," Vance added.

Jillian nodded soberly and indicated the table. "What would you like to know?"

We all sat down.

"What was the name of the person you bought the ice cream from?" I asked.

Vance's notebook appeared in his hand. "Sonya Ladd."

"And she's in Medford?" Vance asked.

"Ashland," Jillian corrected. "She's a very nice single mother who's just trying to make a better life for herself. Don't poke around too hard, Vance. I don't want to make trouble for her."

"Trouble?" I repeated, frowning. "Like what?"

"Oh, let's just say that I already know she doesn't have a commercial kitchen, so technically speaking, she shouldn't be making consumable products for sale. Her ice cream was so good that I knew I had to share it with my customers."

"And she's in Ashland," Vance repeated, as he scribbled notes. "How did you find her? Just stumbled into her store one day?"

"Coffee shop. I was in line for an iced tea and Sonya was in front of me. We got to talking, since the line was long, and she told me she's an amateur confectioner. Naturally, this piqued my curiosity, so I followed her back to her place and she gave me a few samples. The rest, as they say, is history."

"Did she mention anything about using special ingredients?" I asked.

Jillian shook her head. "The only thing she told me was that all her desserts were made with love and the most wholesome organic ingredients she could find."

"Organic," I repeated, frowning. "I'm really starting to dislike that word."

"Stop your fretting," Jillian returned. "You don't need to worry about Sonya. She's an open book. You won't find a more honest person."

"We'd still like to talk to her," I said.

My wife nodded and pulled out her phone. She tapped the display a few times before my own phone announced I had a text. How? By chirping like a cricket. It's a long story. Anyway, just like that, I now had every piece of contact info for Ms. Sonya Ladd that my wife had, all in a few button taps. Honestly, I have no idea how she does it.

"You've got the address?" Vance asked me.

"Apparently. I think we're good to go. Now what? Ask Vino who sold him his ice cream?"

"And gelato," Vance reminded me.

"Right. Gelato, too."

"I figure if we get the names of the sellers, and get enough information from each of them, somewhere down the line we'll find something that links them together."

"I sure hope so," I said.

Vance continued to scroll through screens on his phone. Just then, we heard someone climb the stairs. Hmm, is that how I sounded? Like an asthmatic pachyderm?

Dottie's head appeared. She zeroed in on Jillian and she waved. Then, she saw me and immediately hurried over, throwing her arms around me in the process.

Now, I feel like I should give a little context. Dottie Hanson is the one and only offspring of the late Clara Hanson, PV's late femme fatale. Clara had a way of letting you know what her intentions were, all without her saying a word. Body language, I'm sorry to say, spoke volumes, and Clara's was always screaming at the top of its lungs.

Dottie moved to town not long after her mother had passed away. She smoothly took over the day-to-day operations of her mother's beloved bookstore, A Lazy Afternoon, and seeing how Dottie hadn't known anyone upon arriving, had quickly bonded to both Jillian and me.

The new business owner was in her late twenties, or early thirties. I couldn't tell, and I wasn't about to commit the ultimate taboo by asking a female her age. I may be getting foolish as I get older, but I'm not that far gone, thank you very much. Dottie wore her hair just past her shoulders, and usually had several streaks of color highlighting her otherwise brunette hair. This week, it was pink and orange.

Dottie pulled back, took Jillian's hands in hers, and did a little dance. "You're not going to believe this! It's black! I'm black!"

Our table fell silent as the three of us cocked our heads at the young woman dancing a jig in front of us. My lips quivered as I fought to keep the smile from forming on my face. Dottie looked at me, gave me a quizzical look, and then she must have reviewed that scene in her head. Her face was suddenly redder than a fire truck.

"Omigod, that's not what I meant. *In the!* I'm *in the* black now! A Lazy Afternoon is finally turning a profit, and that's doing everything on my own! I feel like celebrating!"

Jillian clapped her hands together excitedly. "Good for you, Dottie. Didn't I say you could do it from day one?"

"You did, yes," the young woman admitted, offering us a shy smile. "I couldn't have done it without you. So, what's everyone doing here today? Oh, hello Detective Samuelson. I didn't see you there. But, I'm sure you clearly heard me."

Vance nodded. "Afternoon, Ms. Hanson. And yes, I did. I don't think I've ever heard that phrase used in that context before."

Jillian smacked him on the arm. Grinning, and pleased that I wasn't on the receiving end of that strike, I started to smirk when my wife looked at me and gave me a matching slug on the arm. From shoulder to fingertips, my entire arm started tingling, and not in a good way.

"Every time," I groaned, as I tried to will away the effects of having my funny bone thwacked. "And what did I do? I didn't say anything!"

"Yes, but you *thought it*. Men. Dottie, we'll have to celebrate. We'll take you out to dinner tonight. Your choice. Where would you like to go?"

Dottie glanced over at me and I started mouthing words. "Umm, how about Casa de Joe's?"

"That sounds wonderful. We can go tonight, or if there's a day that works better for you?"

Dottie shrugged. "My social calendar is pretty flexible. Wait. You're working on a case, aren't you?"

I nodded. "We are, yes."

"Well, when you, er, that is, if you haven't already, maybe when you ...?"

I looked at Jillian and shrugged. I had no idea what Dottie was asking.

"Corgi clues," my wife whispered.

"What about them?" I asked. Then, it dawned on me. "Oh, I get it. You're asking whether or not I've collected everyone together yet to go over the pictures?"

Dottie nodded eagerly.

"I haven't, not yet. But, I know we're getting close. Tell you what. Today is Monday. I'm going to think optimistically here and say we should be ready to review those pictures in a day or two. Let's shoot for Wednesday evening, all right? And, if something comes up, we can always plan for our typical Friday."

Dottie nodded. "I can't wait! Well, you guys are busy, so I guess I should ..."

Jillian indicated the chair on her right. "Come, join us. You're a business owner. We'd appreciate your input."

Dottie sat so fast that I didn't even see her pull out the chair. "Awesome! What can I do for you?"

We all turned to Vance, who shrugged.

"We need to find out why ice cream is being targeted. First robbery happened here, at Cookbook Nook. It ..."

"Did you know there's another Cookbook Nook?" Dottie suddenly interrupted. "Oh, pardon me. That was rude."

I glanced up. "Another Cookbook Nook? You don't say."

"I *do* say. I found it online."

"Where?" I wanted to know.

"It's somewhere up in northern Idaho. According to their website, they sell the same things you do. Mrs. Anderson? You don't seem too surprised. Did you know about them?"

Jillian nodded. "I think I did, yes. Every so often, I get an email from random strangers, thinking we are them. One of these days, I'll have to reach out to our 'sister' store and compare notes. I'm sorry, Vance. You were saying?"

"I'm saying something doesn't add up. Look at the facts. The ice cream that was stolen from here ended up in a dumpster not far away. On top of which, the guy who stole the ice cream was also found, in that same dumpster."

Jillian sighed. "Ugh. Don't remind me."

"Then, the brother of this thief is also found dead, with a cause of death similar to the first guy."

"It makes me think that they were looking for something in the ice cream, too," I said, "and when they didn't find it, they thought maybe the guy's brother stole it?"

Vance nodded. "My thinking exactly. Then there's Vino's place. Er, Corner Delights. A completely innocent kid is paid ten thousand dollars and encouraged to get the ice cream any way he can. He buys it. But, when delivered, there's clearly something wrong, 'cause the tubs are searched and the ice cream is abandoned. I need to know why. Anyone have any theories?"

"Nothing that hasn't already been considered," I answered. "I maintain they were looking for something inside the ice cream, and they're clearly not finding it."

Vance nodded. "Agreed. Anyone else?"

"Maybe it was missing an ingredient?" Jillian suggested.

Vance shook his head. "According to Barry Foster, the kid who paid for the ice cream, the guy who hired him knew full well which flavors he wanted. That would suggest familiarity with the flavor, don't you think?"

Jillian nodded. "It would. That can't be it."

"Something is *supposed* to be in the ice cream?" Dottie hesitantly suggested.

Jillian looked up. "Like what?"

Dottie shrugged. "I don't know. Like something stolen?"

Vance shook his head. "We'd have heard about it. It's a great idea, though. Well done, Ms. Hanson."

Dottie blushed.

"Anyone else?" my detective friend asked.

Dottie hesitantly raised her hand. "I've got another possibility."

Vance waved her on. "Let's hear it."

"I've been watching this show on television," Dottie began. "It's all about smuggling, and the extremes which bad guys employ in order to hide their drugs. Maybe there was something in the tub that they had managed to remove?"

"We already have asked that," Vance said. "Mr. Foster reported the tubs had been hacked apart by a kitchen knife. Whoever paid him to get the ice cream clearly thought along the same lines."

"Wait," I said, holding up my hand. "Thought along the same lines. That would suggest … wouldn't it suggest he really doesn't know what he's looking for? That he knows there's something he needs to collect, but for whatever the reason, the only information he has is that it has something to do with the ice cream?"

"That tub was destroyed," Vance reminded me. "If there had been something in it, they would have found it."

"What about if it was *on* the tub?" Jillian suggested. "Like a label? Or a concealed memory card?"

"In a freezer?" I asked.

"You know what I mean. Is that even possible?"

Vance shrugged. "At this point, I'll go with anything. I guess it's possible."

I placed a hand over my wife's, on the table, and gave it a squeeze. "Well, we have Sonya's information. Our next step is clear. We need to find out what she's doing with her ice cream that makes it so desirable."

"I know quite a few people in the ice cream industry," Jillian reported. "I'll make some calls and see if I can find anything out. Dottie, when do you have to be back at your store?"

"I've got about forty-five minutes left."

"Great! Would you like to help?"

"I thought you'd never ask."

I looked at my detective friend. "Well? Looks like we need to plan on making a trip to Ashland."

EIGHT

T he aforementioned trip to Ashland didn't take place for two days. Thanks to a rash of graffiti that started appearing in the area, all available police personnel were tasked with finding out who had the *cojones* to tag the police department with a number of brands and symbols. To say that Captain Nelson was less than enthused was a severe understatement. When Vance finally did call, it was early Wednesday morning.

"Hey there, pal. Thought you had dropped off the face of the earth."

"Damn punk kids. They think they can do whatever they want, without worrying about any consequences. Well, when we get our hands on them, they're going to be sorry."

"They marked the police department?" I asked, after he told me what had been targeted. I could only hope Vance would be unable to tell I was smiling.

"It was some quality work," Vance conceded. "They must have been out there for some time."

"Don't you guys have security cameras outside?" I asked.

"We do, but they don't cover everything," Vance said. He let out a sigh. "But, I guaran-damn-tee you they will now. The captain has already put in an order for a much more sophisticated system. This new setup will nearly triple the number of cameras. Our station's not that big, Zack. Every square inch is going to be covered. The captain is not going to let someone do that to him again."

"No idea who it could be?"

"Who else? Just some kids, no doubt. Are you busy? Got some time to run out to Ashland?"

"I'm just skimming through *Spirit of Éire*, doing a bit of self-editing at the moment."

I hadn't announced to anyone that I was even working on the sequel to my bestselling *Heart of Éire*, let alone finished it. In case you didn't know, my Ireland book only came to be because of Vance. As predicted, I heard him gasp once and go silent on me. I waited a few moments before clearing my throat.

"Still with me?"

"Y-you wrote it? Already? H-how? When?"

"I've been working on it for a while now. MCU has been hounding me about it non-stop, but that's something you wouldn't know, 'cause you don't have to deal with my publisher. Yes, it's done, but seeing how well the first one performed, I have to make certain that this one is a worthy sequel. So, I'm being extra cautious. As for how I wrote it so fast, well, the thing practically wrote itself. Every time I finished a chapter, I started thinking about the next, and various ideas would pop into my head. What if I made Tori do *this*? Or, what if *that* happened to the family? Seriously," I continued, tapping the side of my head. "The voices wouldn't shut up. Therefore, instead of trying to suppress them, I let them all play out and wrote them down. The first half of the book was written in this manner."

"Dude, that's … that's amazing."

"Well, color me impressed. I'm hitting the record button. This is Zack Anderson, on the phone with Vance Samuelson, who's about to admit that he's impressed by me, Zack Anderson. Go ahead, caller."

"Oh, ha ha. Smartass. So, care to get some fresh air?"

"Absolutely. Let me go wake up the dogs and, what, should we meet there? Or, did you want to me to drive to your place and hop in your car?"

Vance hesitated. "Well, um, er, I was thinking that, since there's no point in both of us driving, and at the moment, I happened to be closer to you than you are to me, I could head to your place and catch a ride with you."

"Sure, no problem. Let me get my keys."

"Er, Zack?"

"I know that tone of voice. You want something. Out with it, pal. What is it?"

"Is there any way we could take that slick hot rod of yours?"

"The Ruxton? Yeah, I suppose so. If we get

accosted by a mob of people, then you are going to run point. Agreed?"

"I've got my gun. Sure, why not?"

Thirty minutes later, with Sherlock and Watson sitting comfortably in the Ruxton's back seat, I merged onto I-5 South and accelerated. The huge car purred as it surged forward, drawing appreciative looks from everyone we passed. Once we hit cruising speed, Vance eagerly pulled out his notebook and flipped it open.

"Now's as good of a time as ever to tell you."

My curiosity was piqued. "I'm all ears. What's up? Wait. Something happened, didn't it? You have some news?"

Vance grinned a smile that'd make the Cheshire Cat jealous. "I sure do. We have our first link that ties the two thefts together."

"What? Really? Why didn't you open with that?"

"Where's the fun in that? Now, listen. We already have the name of the lady who supplied the ice cream to Jillian, remember?"

"Ms. Sonya Ladd. I remember."

"I finally heard back from Vino last night. Looks like he had a heart-to-heart with his nephews. He mentioned to you he didn't remember making two of those missing tubs of ice cream, remember?"

"I do, yes."

"Well, one of the nephews, Tommaso, let it slip he purchased several tubs of a specialty ice cream. He thought it'd be a great fit for the store. He'd slipped them in the display when Vino wasn't watching. And, from what Vino was able to get out of Tommaso, this ice cream came from a person he met while he was visiting—wait for it!—Ashland."

"Ashland? No way. Did he confirm it was the same lady?"

"He didn't remember the name," Vance said, "but in proper male fashion, he remembered her physical appearance."

"If you say what I think you're gonna say, then you'll have to remind me to personally pop that chauvinistic piece of work right on the nose."

"You sound like Tori," Vance chuckled. "No, the only thing he remembered was a woman about the same age as him, which I'm guessing is anywhere from early to late thirties. Let's see. She has black, shoulder-length hair, is slim, and has a tattoo sleeve on her left arm."

"And we probably don't know what Sonya Ladd looks like, do we?" I guessed.

"Not yet we don't. That's what we're going to find out."

"I honestly don't understand this fascination with ice cream," I admitted, a few minutes later. We were presently about ten miles south of Medford, and according to the signs, had another ten or so to go until we made it to Ashland. "I know it's good during the summer, but come on. I've yet to taste a flavor so damn good that I'd be willing to kill for it."

"You're a good person," Vance reminded me.

"You have a good sense of what's right and wrong. Not everyone does, buddy."

"If Sonya Ladd *is* the missing link between these two thefts, what do you hope to find?"

Vance shrugged. "I really don't know. Maybe a name? Or, maybe the name of an obscure store where she purchases all of her ingredients? Maybe there's some special way she makes everything? This is too coincidental, Zack. The answer is out there. It's up to us to find it."

Oh, the answer would become clear, all right, only it'd be no thanks to us. More on that later.

As we approached our exit and I activated the turn signal, Vance suddenly looked at me and raised an eyebrow.

"What?" I asked.

"Have you found one yet?"

"Found one *what*?"

"A name, of course. I know you and Jillian have been trying to come up with suitable names for your new house. Are there any contenders?"

You *did* know that's what Jillian and I have been doing, right? I do know that it's not common for people to name their homes here, in the States. However, Jillian is a born-again romantic. She loves the idea of having a name for her home. I'm also convinced that's why she loves Carnation Cottage so much. It's a historic house in PV, and like all of them, they have their own names.

"We've tried out quite a variety," I told my friend. "I've used some of my favorite movies, and she, of course, has tried naming it after some flower. Oh, and some fancy French words. I don't know, man. I want it to be unique. I want it to be *us*. I'm hoping that when we *do* stumble across the right name, we'll both know it." Fingers crossed it wouldn't take too long.

"Here we go," Vance was saying. "Turn right here. Now, at the next intersection, make a left. Oh, get into the left lane. What we're looking for will be on our left. What? What is it?"

I was staring at my friend as though he had sprouted a second head. "You've been talking to Jillian," I accused.

"She might've given me a few pieces of advice when it comes to being your navigator. She told me you have a very analytical brain, so keep the instructions short and precise, and we'll get along just fine. I have to say, it's certainly beats reliving the Firemen Fiasco."

I glared at my friend. "That happened last Christmas. Besides, you tampered with my phone and you *know it*."

"It's nothing to worry about," Vance teased. "Didn't those friendly firemen come to your rescue?"

"True, they did. But, that was after I got so freakin' turned around that I sank my Jeep into several feet of sludge. They were laughing so damn hard it's a wonder any of them could see straight. And I know you told them to be ready. How else could they have gotten there in less than two minutes?"

"It's a small town?" Vance guessed, between snorts of laughter.

"Just you wait. I'll find a way to get even *and* post it online."

"It's water under the bridge," Vance insisted. "Now, where were we?"

"Aside from plotting revenge?"

"Yeah, yeah. Aside from that."

"I think I see where we're going. Humboldt Street? The turn is coming. Jillian said the fourth house on the left is the one we want."

"It's not much to look at, is it?" Vance said, as we came to a stop a few minutes later. "Looks like this thing was built at least fifty years ago."

I was silent as I studied the house. Worn wood shingles for siding, paint peeling from the trim around the windows, and several window screens were sagging in their frames. Yes, this was a house that had seen better days, but then again, everything else looked good. Flowerbeds were weeded and had bright, colorful flowers. A black hose was coiled neatly around a water faucet. The house had a small, fenced-in grass yard in front, and that lawn looked healthier—and greener—than any of the others, despite having weeds growing through the cracks in the cement sidewalk. Whoever lived here was taking care of the property as best as they could.

An older yellow Labrador, who had been stretched out on the steps leading up to the front door, lazily got to his feet and walked over to us. The friendly muzzle was thrust into my hand, and after a few scratches, the dog gave me a cursory lick in greeting, before the process was repeated with Vance. Surprised that my own two dogs hadn't lost their minds had me looking down to judge their reactions. Sherlock and Watson were watching the much larger newcomer, but thankfully, their body language suggested there was nothing to fear here.

The yellow dog must've caught their scent because his snout dropped until he was staring at the two of them from the other side of the chain link fence. The corgis approached, sniffed noses, and then lost interest.

"Think they'll all get along?" Vance asked, with his hand resting on the gate's latch.

"No one has so much as growled at one another. I think everyone is okay with one another."

Vance nodded and slipped the catch up, allowing the gate to open. The Labrador waited patiently for the four of us to enter his yard before nuzzling our sides, seeking attention. Vance offered the big dog a biscuit, and then caught sight of the two corgis. Both sat the moment a treat made an appearance. Laughing, Vance gave each of them a biscuit, too.

"Do you always walk around with a pocket full of dog treats?" I wanted to know. "You always seem to have them."

Vance held up his right hand and formed an *O*.

"Zero times, pal. That's how many times I've been bitten by a dog. It's amazing how little it takes to get on a dog's good side. So, I come prepared."

The front door opened and we were suddenly face-to-face with a brunette woman wearing a blue turtleneck sweater, black jeans, and a stained white apron. Her hair was pulled up into a ponytail and the sleeves of her sweater had been pushed back, to her elbows. Her left arm was covered with tattoos.

"Oh, hello. I didn't know we had visitors. Thanks a lot, Markus. You could've barked, you know. Hi, I'm Sonya. Is there something I can help you with today?"

Vance held up his identification. "Detective Samuelson, PVPD. This is Zack Anderson. Down there are Sherlock and Watson."

"Corgis! I don't see many of those around here. Markus hasn't been a pest, has he?"

"They're getting along just fine," Vance reported. "Ms. Ladd? Do you have a couple of minutes? We'd like to ask you a few questions."

"I never told you my last name," Sonya said, frowning. "Oh, heavens above. What has that jackass accused me of this time?"

My detective friend looked up. "Would you run that by me one more time? Are you in danger?"

"Of being thrown in jail," Sonya scowled. "Are you married?"

"Yes."

"Oh, I'm sorry."

"We're both married," I added.

"Umm, to each other?"

Vance and I looked at each other.

"What? No. My wife's name is Tori. His is Jillian."

Sonya's frown disappeared. "Wait. You said you're from Pomme Valley. And his wife's name is Jillian? Would this be the same Jillian that I met not that long ago?"

I nodded. "One and the same. She gave us your contact information."

Sonya nodded solemnly. "Well, at least this doesn't sound like it involves Patrick in any way, shape, or form."

"Patrick?" Vance echoed.

"My ex. The less said about him, the better. Come on in. Let's get this over with."

"Are you okay with the dogs coming in?" I asked.

Sonya nodded. "Of course."

We followed Sonya up the porch and into her house. Once the door was closed behind us, she ushered us through the house's tiny living room into its even smaller kitchen. The kitchen may have been small, but Sonya was using every square inch of space. Racks of cookies were cooling on the stove. Several types of dough were in various bowls, with plastic wrap over them, as they waited to proof. The small sink had various baking utensils and bowls, stacked neatly to the side, waiting their turn to be cleaned.

"This is some operation you have here," Vance began. "The reason for our visit is ..."

"Look, I know, all right?" Sonya interrupted, with a sigh.

"You know what?" Vance asked.

"I know what you're doing here. Just tell me how long I have."

"How long you have for *what*?" I asked.

"Before you shut me down," Sonya said, as she washed her hands in the sink and turned around to face us. A few moments later, she folded her arms across her chest. "All I ask is that you let me fill the orders that I currently have. Please understand, my customers are relying on me. I can't let them down."

Vance held up his hands in a time-out gesture. "What do you think we're here for?"

"This isn't a commercial kitchen," Sonya said, growing irritated. "It's just not in the budget. So, I make do with what I have. It's all I can do."

"I'm here about ice cream," Vance clarified.

"Ice cream?" Sonya repeated, confused. "You're not here to shut me down?"

"I wasn't planning on it. Actually, I couldn't, even if I wanted to. I'm out of my jurisdiction. We were just hoping we could get some information about the ice cream you sold Jillian Anderson."

"His wife?" Sonya said, as she pointed a finger at me. "I remember Mrs. Anderson. She was nice. She knew I had no business doing what I'm doing from my kitchen, but she made a purchase anyway.

What about the ice cream? Who cares about ice cream? I have nothing to do with it once it goes out that door."

"You've heard about the two robberies?" Vance asked. "One in PV and the other here, in Medford?"

"I'm too busy to pay attention to the news," Sonya exclaimed. "If I don't work, I don't get paid. Since Mrs. Anderson was here, I've made three cakes, five dozen cupcakes, and eight dozen cookies, and I know that's all from her influence. Now, if one of my customers has filed a complaint, all I ask is that you tell me which one. I make sure all my customers are completely happy when they walk out my door."

"No one has filed anything on you," Vance reiterated. "We're only here to ask you about the ice cream you made. Er, you *do* remember the several tubs of ice cream you sold, don't you?"

Sonya visibly calmed. "I do, yes. I hope you don't want more. To be honest, I think I'm going to give up ice cream. It's just not worth the effort. So, what do you want to know?"

Vance turned to me. "Do you remember what flavor Jillian had?"

I fired off a quick text. Jillian's answer came back almost as quickly.

"She had two: *Celebration* and *Hawaiian Sunrise*. The latter was the one that was taken."

Sonya perked up. "Hold up. Someone stole my *Hawaiian Sunrise*? She didn't get to sell it?"

"Jillian said there wasn't much that had sold,

but it was also too early to tell how well it was going to perform. That tub, and the one she had in storage, was stolen."

"I only sold her the two," Sonya recalled. "It was all I made of that flavor. Wait. *Celebration* was left alone? But … that doesn't make any sense!"

"And now you know why we're here," Vance stated. My pal's no-nonsense police voice was now being used. "Did you also provide product to a local ice cream shop by the name of Corner Delights?"

"I have no idea," Sonya admitted.

"Think," I urged. "This would have been another large purchase. This would have been another couple of tubs being sold, to the same guy."

Sonya nodded. "I *do* remember someone like that. Young, thin, wore a lot of jewelry. Italian, I think."

"That'd be Tommaso," I said, smiling.

Sonya's face paled. "Wait. Is that the other business that was robbed? And my ice cream … it was stolen? Again?"

Vance nodded. "Yes. Do you have any idea why?"

Sonya sank down onto the closest chair. In this case, it was a stool. "Why? Who would want that much ice cream? And why not just steal it from here?"

"You definitely don't want that kind of trouble here," Vance told her, as gently as he could.

"The hell with that," Sonya snapped. "I

would've mopped the floor with him. Just let someone try to pull that crap on me. What? I don't look like I can take care of myself? I've been a trained kickboxer for over a year now. I can take care of myself."

"I have no doubt you can," I said, holding out my fist. Sonya noticed and thumped it good with hers. In fact, I think I bruised a few knuckles in the process. "However, think, Sonya. Is there anything about your ice cream that stands out? Where did you get the ingredients? How was it made? Was there some type of proprietary process you employed to make all this happen?"

"Everything I used I bought from the local grocery store," Sonya admitted. "I'd like to say that I imported ingredients and supplies from various countries, but let's be honest. Do I look like someone who'd do that? And how did I make it? I have a little countertop model ice cream maker. It took a long time to come up with that much product. That's why I got out of the ice cream business. It was simply too much time and effort to make. It wasn't worth it. So, to answer your question, why would someone steal it? Well, not to toot my own horn, but it's really friggin' good ice cream."

I grinned. Something about this lady made me smile. Here she was, a single mother, just trying to earn a living. And, she wasn't about to take any guff from anyone. You have to admire that in a woman.

"Look, would it make you two feel any better if I run you through how I made it?" Sonya asked.

Vance looked at me, intent on seeing if I had any objections to observing the process. I gave him a quick nod of my head. "It would, thanks."

"That's why you never say never," Sonya muttered, as she moved between various cabinets and began pulling out an assortment of utensils. "Not two days ago I said I'd never make another batch of ice cream, yet here I am, about to make another. Well, this time, it'll be something simple. You. Mr. Anderson. What is your wife's favorite flavor?"

Vance looked curiously at me when I didn't have an immediate answer.

"Oh, man. I know this. Hold on a second."

"No texting," Vance ordered, as he grinned at me.

"Let's see. I know she loves chocolate. Oh! Mint chocolate chip! That's her favorite."

"I don't know how to make mint," Sonya confessed, "but I do make a mean triple chocolate flavor. I called it *Trifecta*. Dark chocolate ice cream with a fudge swirl and bits of brownies thrown in. Wait. Let me see if I … yep, there we go. I still have some brownies left over. Okay, pay attention."

I might not have been a confectioner, nor have I ever attempted to make a homemade ice cream, but even I could see that there really wasn't anything special to Sonya's technique. She mixed up the base, added it to the soft serve machine, and in less than thirty minutes, a rich chocolate dessert was dispensed out of Sonya's counter-top ice cream maker. But, as she was dispensing the product, I saw her grab what looked like a big pastry bag, minus the metal tip, and squirt in the ribbon of fudge. At the same time, she tossed in handfuls of chopped up pieces of brownies. Once the quart-sized plastic container was full, she snapped on a lid, peeled a sticker off a sheet found in a nearby binder, and wrote the name of the flavor on the label. She handed it to me with a smile.

"There you go. That's all there is to it."

"How much do I owe you?" I asked, pulling out my wallet.

"It's on the house."

"Oh, no you don't. Give me a number."

"It's. On. The. House."

"Fine. You win."

Smiling victoriously, Sonya slipped my quart of ice cream into a white plastic sack and handed it to me.

"If there's anything else I can do for you guys, just let me know, okay? And Mr. Anderson? If Mrs. Anderson would ever like some more ice cream, well, I'd make it. For her."

"You just said you didn't want to make anymore," I pointed out.

"And I said I'd do it ... *for her*."

"I'll let her know." I made eye contact with Vance and tilted my head toward the door. My friend shrugged and nodded. "Sherlock? Watson? Let's head for ... guys? What are you doing? Let's go, huh?"

The corgis were sitting so still they looked like they were posing for pictures. Both, I might add, were staring at something off to the left. What was over there? A couple of folding chairs.

"What are they looking at?" Vance asked, eager to see what the dogs had located.

"What's going on?" Sonya asked. "What are your dogs doing?"

"What are they staring at?" Vance wanted to know. He slowly walked around me and the dogs and approached the chairs. He stooped to pick something up. "This? Come on, guys. This can't be what you want."

The dogs watched Vance as he slowly walked around the room. Neither corgi blinked.

"What do you have there?" I wanted to know.

"It's just a hat," Vance answered. "A typical baseball hat."

"It's my son's," Sonya said, once she caught sight of it. "It belongs to Trevor. I'm surprised he left that here. He never goes anywhere without it."

On the hat's front panel was a picture of a very famous celebrity, one who started his career as a professional wrestler. Obviously, Trevor was a fan. Eyeing the dogs, I sighed. Pulling out my phone, I snapped a picture, which resulted in the dogs rising to their feet and ignoring the rest of us.

Vance, however, had his notebook back out.

"I'm sorry, I should have thought to ask about your kid. This Trevor, how old is he?"

"He has absolutely nothing to do with what I do in my kitchen," Sonya declared, growing defensive.

"I know that, Ms. Ladd. I'm here to collect information. We still need to figure out why thieves are targeting your creations. I would think you'd want us to find out who's behind these thefts just as soon as possible."

"You're right, I'm sorry. I'm so used to pointing out that my ex is … wait. Have you looked into Patrick? If ever there was someone who wanted to cause problems for me, it'd be him."

"Patrick," Vance repeated, as he added the name to his notes. "Last name?"

"You don't think it's Ladd?"

Vance shook his head. "From the little time I've spent with you, I figure the last thing you'd want is to keep his name. So, I'm guessing Ladd is your maiden name?"

Sonya nodded. "You're a good detective."

"No, I'm a *great* detective," Vance corrected, with a smile. "What is Patrick's last name?"

"Hummel."

"And what does Patrick Hummel do for a living?" Vance inquired.

"Businessman. He runs his own shop on the other side of Medford."

"What kind of shop?" Vance inquired.

"A pawn shop," Sonya said, shrugging. "He makes a killing. Personally, I could never do that to people."

Vance was scribbling like crazy. Sonya noticed, and volunteered the pawn shop's address. Could this be the mastermind behind the thefts?

"While Vance is busy writing that down, Sonya, let me ask you something. Do backpacks, rainbows, insects, or sunglasses mean anything to you?"

Sonya gave me a look which suggested she thought I wasn't playing with a full deck. "Aside from naming objects that everyone uses on a daily basis, I can't see how any of that is relevant."

"And rainbows?" I prompted.

Sonya shrugged. "Maybe it's just another way of saying we should all be in a good mood? Why do you ask about these things?"

I sighed and looked at the dogs. Sherlock and Watson were staring at the door, eager to leave.

"Oh, it's nothing. I was just checking. Vance? Got everything you need?"

"I think so. Ms. Ladd, thank you for your cooperation."

"Anytime, detective. Mr. Anderson? Get that in the freezer soon, or plan on getting a straw."

I laughed and nodded.

Back on the road, Vance pulled out his cell and called the station. He relayed what we had just learned about Sonya Ladd, and asked them to check into one Patrick Hummel. It was at this time that Vance tapped the speaker button on his phone and turned up the volume.

"I can relay the information we have at hand," I heard Julie's voice say. "Sonya Ladd. Divorced, one child. She's had a string of businesses, all legit. Current occupation says chef, but doesn't list a restaurant."

"She's self-employed," Vance relayed.

"Acknowledged. There are no priors, and her license comes back fine."

Vance nodded. "Thought as much. Anything on her ex, Patrick Hummel?"

"Let me clear the screen and start over. Okay, let's see. Owner of Grab and Go Pawn. Divorced, one child, obviously. Registered owner of three guns. Several priors, including aggravated assault and possession of stolen items. Captain Nelson is here. He wants to know if this is a person of interest in your case?"

"He's now at the top of the list."

"Roger that. The captain just said he's going to put out an APB for him. Good job, Vance. Say hello to Zack for me."

"Will do, Jules. Thanks." Once the call was terminated, Vance held up a fist. "That worked out better than I thought! Nicely done, buddy. We have our first suspect!"

In less than twenty-four hours, we were going to learn that not only did we not have the right guy, we weren't even in the right ballpark.

NINE

A round one o'clock the following afternoon, I was back in my car and on a return trip to Ashland. Why? Well, nothing so far today has made any sense to me, so let me start from the beginning.

My wife and I were having a lovely breakfast together at Carnation Cottage when my phone gave me its customary text message chirp. Checking the display, I saw that Vance was letting me know that Patrick Hummel wasn't our guy. To say I was disappointed would be an understatement.

Sonya Ladd's ex-husband, unfortunately for us, had a cast-iron alibi: he wasn't in town during either of the robberies. Patrick had been attending some type of gun expo in Portland, and had the receipts from his hotel to prove it. Vance called in a couple of favors and was able to get the hotel to send over security footage confirming Hummel's story.

The interview, Vance told me later, lasted nearly an hour. No one clearly believed anything the pawn store owner was saying, so as each fact came out, it was checked. And double-checked. For every question, Hummel had a legitimate answer.

As expected, Vance asked about Patrick's rap sheet, which included charges of aggravated assault and possession of stolen property. When confronted with this, Patrick Hummel easily smiled at my detective friend and smoothly explained that he had been assaulted by a couple who were high as kites. When he had politely, but firmly, rebuffed the woman's advances, the husband inexplicably became enraged. The husband grabbed a bat from a nearby wall rack and smashed several displays before Hummel had been able to defuse the situation. And by defuse, Vance explained later, he meant catching the bat in mid-swing, smashing his forearm through it, which broke the bat, and drop-kicking the hapless individual through the front window.

"He is an experienced mixed martial artist," Vance explained, when we met up later in the morning. "However, charges were pressed, and Patrick took the heat."

"Do you believe him?" I had asked.

"Do you know what? I do. This guy is smart. He … oh! You didn't hear the best part."

"By all means, tell me the best part," I urged, giving him a grin.

"I think he's still in love with his wife."

"You're kidding. How'd you work that out?"

"He had receipts for everything he's done to her house. Whenever she has a problem with *anything*, she calls him and he hurries over. Garbage disposal, painting, or automobile repair, when she calls, he comes running."

"He's hoping to reconcile," I said, thinking hard. "Did he say whether or not Sonya was interested?"

"Does it matter?" Vance countered.

"I guess not. Either way you look at it, I don't see how either of them would have the motive to pull off something like this."

"Agreed."

"What about Hummel's other charge?" I wanted to know.

"Possession of stolen items?" Vance asked. "I posed that same question to him. Want to know what he said? *Show me a pawn shop owner who hasn't ever come into contact with stolen property.* I had to hand it to him. It made sense."

"That's just swell," I groaned. "Our lead suspect not only lacks the motivation to be our guy, but has a rock-solid alibi, so he's definitely not the one who pulled this off. Do you know where that leaves us?"

"With diddly squat," Vance scowled. "I thought for certain we had finally caught a break, pal. Captain Nelson stopped by here earlier, when I was in with Hummel. I'm told he was in a pleasant mood. He must've thought we found our guy, too. I sure as hell don't want to be the one to tell him we've got the wrong man."

Sherlock and Watson perked up. They both started wiggling with anticipation. That could only mean they spotted someone, and that particular person was on their way over.

"Man your battle stations," I said, under my breath. "I think you said his name too many times. The captain is headed this way."

"I'm screwed, pal."

"Duck down."

"What?"

"Duck down! Hurry! He's only seen me."

I didn't think he'd do it. Vance purposely dropped his pen and ducked to retrieve it. Moments later, Captain Nelson poked his head through the door.

"Anderson? I thought I heard Detective Samuelson in here."

"You just missed him. He got a phone call, and I don't think he was eager to answer it. At least, he didn't want to take it in front of me."

"Any idea who it was?" the captain inquired.

Thinking fast, I fought the urge to smile. "Well, to tell the truth, sir, I've overheard him talking to his wife about getting tickets to some performing arts center. He seemed embarrassed when he thought I could be listening. Something about live performances?"

"It wasn't the Craterian Theater at the Collier Center, was it?" the captain asked, becoming interested.

The only reason I knew anything about this particular theater was because Jillian had been dropping some not-so-subtle hints about what she'd like to do for her birthday.

I snapped my fingers and nodded. "That was the one."

"I didn't know Samuelson enjoyed the opera. My wife loves to go, but I'm honestly not that big of a fan. It would be nice to go with someone who enjoys it. It'd make her happy. Remind me to ask him about it the next time I see him."

"Oh, you got it, sir. Scout's honor."

"Perfect. Sherlock, Watson, keep up the good work."

Both corgis were pulling at the leash, eager to go say hello to the captain. Once they had, Captain Nelson nodded at me and left.

Vance's head popped up, over the desk, like a prairie dog emerging from its den. "What have you gotten me into? Opera? Are you insane?"

"Oh, it gets better," I laughed. "Looks like you and Tori are gonna double-date with the captain and his wife."

Vance fixed me with a stare. "Of course you know, this means *war*."

I fought to keep the smirk from my face. "Hey, I helped you out. You're welcome."

"By telling the captain I like opera? Seriously?"

"You'll thank me later."

"We'll see, buddy. We'll see. Grievances aside, I'm forced to reconsider Ms. Ladd as a suspect."

"I just don't see her as a suspect," I admitted. "She doesn't strike me as the type. Sonya is a single mother trying to make ends meet in any way she can."

Vance suddenly looked up, all traces of annoyance disappearing in a flash. "Say that again."

"Hmm? She's just trying to make ends meet."

"No, before that."

"Umm, she doesn't strike me as the type? Is that what you want me to say?"

Vance shook his head. "You said she's a mother. What do we know about her kid?"

I held up my hands. "Nothing, actually."

Vance sat back down at his desk and woke up his computer. After typing a search string into his computer's database, he fell silent as he read what the computer found.

"Sonya Ladd. Divorced, ex is Patrick Hummel. Yeah, yeah, we know this already. Here we go. One son, named Trevor Hummel. Lives with his mother."

"How old?" I asked.

"Sixteen. Wow. I didn't think Sonya looked old enough to have a sixteen-year-old son."

"That makes two of us," I agreed. "What does it say about him? Does he have a record?"

Vance did some more typing. "Uh, no. He's clean. Damn. So much for that theory."

My phone chose that time to start ringing. "It's Jillian. Excuse me a sec. Hi, Jillian." I put the call on speakerphone and set it on Vance's desk.

"Are you busy?" Jillian asked.

I looked over at Vance, who shook his head. "I'm

just finishing up here, at the station. What's up? Are you all right?"

"I'm fine, thank you for asking. I was hoping I could get you to go on another road trip for me."

"Oh? Where to?"

"Ashland. I just heard from Sonya Ladd. She ... what is it?"

"Oh, nothing," I said. "I don't know how you do it. I was careful this time. I didn't make a noise. It's almost like you knew we were just talking about her."

"You and Vance? Oh, I know. I heard you both. You both are heavy breathers. When I mentioned Ashland, you two held your breath."

"No, I didn't," Vance mumbled.

"Did not," I said, at the same time.

"Mm-hm. So, would you run down there for me, Zachary? Swing by here first, so you can borrow the large ice chest. I bought two more tubs of ice cream and I don't want them melting on the way back."

"From Sonya?" I asked, frowning. "She told us she was done with ice cream, that it wasn't worth the time and effort. Then again, she did mention she'd do it again for you."

"She told me the same thing," Jillian confessed. "She said she felt bad that Cookbook Nook was burglarized. Even though she didn't have anything to do with the theft, she really wants me to try again to sell her product. So, she's giving it a final go."

Vance's hand snaked out and tapped my phone's display, muting the call. "What are the chances our ice cream bandit will strike again? Do you think Jillian knows she's placing herself in danger?"

"The thought had crossed her mind," Jillian's voice said, from my phone. "I assume you tried to mute the call? Well, you didn't hit the right button."

Vance's face colored. "Sorry, Jillian. Are you sure you want to do this?"

"Positive. What do they say about lightning? That it never strikes the same place twice?"

"Mathematically speaking, it's also possible to win the lottery three times in a row," I argued.

"That's a fair point," my wife admitted. "Look, I get the impression she needs the money. So, this is a risk I'm willing to take. Now, would you be a dear and pick them up for me?"

"Fine, I'll do it. I'll be more than happy to get the Ruxton back on the freeway."

"You have Sherlock and Watson with you, right?"

"Yes."

"Good. They'll love spending more time with you."

It took over an hour of solid driving to make it down to Ashland, pick up the ice cream, and head back to town. I'm thankful to say that the dogs were quiet the entire time. Well, wait a moment.

That's not entirely true. They did perk up once I had parked in front of Sonya's house, but I figure that didn't count since they'd already been here once before. Neither barked, by the way.

Gone Nutty. Of the two flavors I knew I was transporting back to PV, one of them was called Gone Nutty. According to what Sonya had told me, it was a peanut butter flavored ice cream with a marshmallow ribbon and chunks of peanut butter cookie dough. I think I was drooling before she finished her description. Of the second, however, she wouldn't tell me what it was. She said it was a surprise *and* an experiment. Therefore, I could only assume it was something I wouldn't touch with a ten-foot pole.

Once I had parked my car in the alley behind Cookbook Nook, and Sydney had taken over watching the dogs, I took the tubs of ice cream upstairs, to Jillian's little café.

"How did they fare?" my wife asked.

"Just fine. Neither barked at all the entire trip."

"No, the ice cream. How'd they do on the trip back? Are they soft?"

I gently squeezed the large container of ice cream. "Yes."

"I made some room for you. That little chest freezer should have enough space to store the tubs. Once you put them away, would you give me a hand?"

"Sure." Once the tubs were chilling in the freezer, I returned to Jillian's side. "What's on your mind? What can I do?"

"Would you check all these tables for me? I just realized that most are wobbly. I think it might have something to do with the break-in. Maybe the bases were loosened when they were all tipped over?"

"Do you have any tools here?"

"I have a small tool box behind the counter, just below the cash register."

I nodded. "Perfect. Okay, let's see. Wow, really? All of these tools have flowers on them."

"They're pretty, aren't they?"

"Pretty tools," I mumbled, sighing heavily. "What's this world coming to?" I took the wrench and the two screwdrivers and began inspecting the tables. "Yep, you're right. The table's base is secured to the top by four bolts. Looks like their little tumble loosened them up a bit. I've got this."

"Thank you, Zachary."

Nearly an hour later, all of the café's small tables were ready for business. I checked the chairs, although there wasn't anything I could do for them even if I *did* find something amiss. The only thing holding those patio chairs together were some heavy-duty welds, and a welder I am *not*.

I heard a commotion behind me and saw that Jillian was in the process of unsealing the tubs of ice cream and placing them in the tiny glass-topped freezer. She held up a cup and smiled at me.

"Would you like to try some? This must be the

Gone Nutty flavor. From the sounds of it, it'll be right up your alley."

"I thought you'd never ask. Let's see. Mmm, that one is a winner, my dear. Peanut butter and marshmallow? With cookie dough interspersed throughout? Oh, man. You'd better keep that stuff away from me. Did you try it?"

"I'm with you," my wife told me. "I like it. Let's try the other one. This one is called Red Dawn."

I looked at the open tub and whistled. That had to be the darkest, deepest, *reddest* ice cream I have ever seen.

"What's in it?" I asked, as I reached out to take the proffered cup.

Jillian was holding out the second ice cream, but also reading from a sheet of paper that must contain notes about the flavors and ingredients used. She suddenly let out a cry of alarm and jerked the cup away from me.

"What gives?" I wanted to know.

"Oh, you don't want to try this one. Trust me."

My hand dropped. "I do. Implicitly. Okay, I'll bite. What's in it?"

"Beets."

My nose wrinkled. "You're kidding. She made a beet-flavored ice cream? Good God, why?"

"It says here that Red Dawn is a beet-flavored ice cream with carob sprinkles."

"Beets and carrots. That's wrong on so many levels."

"Carob, not carrots."

"Carob? As in, the fake chocolate?"

Jillian nodded. "Oh, I see where she's going with this. This is a vegan recipe. I will say those are some bold choices."

"Y-you're not going to try it, are you?" I stammered in protest. "Come on, there's no way you could like that unnatural mix of flavors."

"Oh, don't be so melodramatic. How bad could it be? Let's see. Well, I can certainly taste the beets. I can't say I'm too big of a fan, but it's actually better than I thought. I haven't tasted any of the carob yet. Here we go. This bite has some. Let's see. Wow, that doesn't taste like carob at all. Maybe I've grown too accustomed to chocolate? Let me try a few other bites. Hmm. I think …"

Jillian trailed off, which caused me to look up from the chair I had been inspecting. The first thing I noticed was that her face had become pale. She even sounded like she was out of breath. What was going on?

"Are you okay?" I asked, growing alarmed. Much to my dismay, my lovely wife shook her head no. I was on my feet in a flash and managed to get to her before she stumbled. "What is it? What's going on?"

"It's getting hard to breathe," Jillian whispered.

My phone was out and I hit the dreaded emergency button. I told the dispatcher the moment they got on the line that I needed an ambulance and then hung up, only briefly realizing I had just spoken with Julie, at the police station.

Pomme Valley may be a small town, but one thing was for certain, the residents looked out for one another. I don't know who Julie called, or how she phrased it, but we had EMTs rushing through Cookbook Nook's front door in less than two minutes.

"Up here!" I called. "Sydney, if you can hear me, please keep the dogs out of the way!"

"What's going on, Mr. Anderson?" the young manager asked in a shaky voice.

"We don't know. Not yet."

I was ushered aside as the first EMT arrived upstairs, holding a huge orange tackle-box.

"Holy cow, it's true," one of the medics said. "Someone said our patient was Jillian Anderson, but I didn't believe them. What happened?"

I pointed at the display of ice cream. "Everything was fine until she ate some of that ice cream. Then, it was straight downhill."

The second EMT briefly turned to look at the display case before slipping an oxygen mask over Jillian's nose.

"Mrs. Anderson? Stay with me. Keep focused."

"Zack! Jillian!" a new voice bellowed. Someone was coming up the stairs, two at a time. It was Vance, and he looked as scared as I felt. "What's going on? What happened?"

"That damn ice cream," I scowled. "She sampled the red one and had some type of reaction to it."

Vance's face hardened. "Is this part of the batch

you guys just got from Ashland?"

I nodded. "That's it. I don't care what Medford says. I'm bringing that Sonya woman in. This is just too coincidental."

"You'll get no arguments from me, pal."

"Zachary?" a weak voice said.

I hurried to my wife's side. "Don't try to talk. Save your strength."

Jillian's lovely green eyes found mine. I saw the pain behind her smile and silently vowed to personally beat the snot out of whoever was responsible. She raised a shaky arm and pointed at her café.

"Please. Pull it."

"What, the ice cream? Consider it done. I'll throw the damn stuff away myself."

I felt a hand on my shoulder.

"You go with her," Vance told me. "I'll take care of this. In fact, with your permission, I'd like to have that ice cream tested. If something got her sick, then I'd like to know what. And don't worry about Sherlock and Watson."

"You have my full permission," I told my friend. "And thanks."

Have you ever ridden in the back of an ambulance? I mean, not as the patient, but as a concerned family member? Let me tell you something. It was not pleasant. Every turn and every bump in the road had me cursing silently to myself as I saw Jillian's face wince with pain. I asked the paramedics if there was something they could give her, but they unfortunately told me no. Since they weren't sure what she had ingested that was causing so many problems, they had to hold off administering any type of medication until they knew for certain what they were dealing with. I guess I could see their point of view. It didn't make it any easier, though.

"Don't blame Sonya for this," I heard Jillian whisper.

I leaned forward and took her hand in my own. "It's kinda hard not to point the finger at her. You ate that nasty beet crap and *BAM!* Instant problems."

One of the paramedics looked up. "What was that? She ate some beets?"

I nodded. "We were trying out some new flavors in her café, and that included this beet-flavored ice cream. Coincidentally, it's the one I didn't try, and I'm not showing any signs of problems. Whatever's causing this is in that ice cream."

"There's no proof," Jillian insisted. "It was bad timing, that's all."

"You're the one who told me to pull the ice cream so no one else could eat it," I reminded her.

"Just a precaution."

"Is she allergic to beets?" the EMT asked.

"I've seen her eat them before without any problems. Other than it being some nasty crap I wouldn't eat even if my life depended on it, that is. The point is, she likes it, and has eaten it in the past. I don't see why it'd be a problem now."

"It could have been the peanut butter flavor," my wife insisted.

"I thought you said it wasn't the ice cream," I said.

"You know what I mean."

"That ice cream needs to be tested," the paramedic told me.

"We're way ahead of you. My friend is a detective on the police force. He's having both flavors tested."

"Good. Will you let us know when the test results are in?"

I nodded. "Count on it."

Two hours later, I was sitting at Jillian's bedside while she slept. Her stomach had been pumped, she had been besieged by machines that looked as though they were borrowed from sci-fi movies, and submitted to practically every test suggested by the doctors. Blood was taken, x-rays were shot, and I think I heard them order an MRI.

In the meantime, my cell was ringing off the hook. When I said before that Jillian knew everyone in Pomme Valley, I wasn't kidding. Everyone from the mayor to the high school principal sent their well-wishes, but because Jillian's phone was currently off, I was next in line for the barrage of messages. As I mentioned earlier, my cell phone was programmed to chirp like a cricket should I get a text call. Well, you'd think the room we were in was getting overrun by insects.

After the fifth message in as many minutes, I ended up silencing my phone.

My phone buzzed again. Sighing, I glanced at the display. This time, I saw Vance's name.

SHE OK?

I told him that she had her stomach pumped, so whatever had been affecting her had been removed. She was stable, and she was resting.

TEST RESULTS IN. YOU SITTING DOWN?

THAT WAS QUICK. THOUGHT IT'D TAKE LONGER.

Vance's reply made my blood run cold.

DIDN'T SAY LAB RESULTS, I SAID TEST RESULTS. SOMEONE SUGGESTED WE RUN A FEW FIELD TESTS ON THE ICE CREAM. ZACK, IT TESTED POSITIVE FOR FENTANYL.

I may not be a cop, and know absolutely nothing about drugs, but I *have* heard of fentanyl and the dangers it poses. What the blazes was it doing in ice cream? Had Jillian's ice cream been deliberately sabotaged? Was Sonya Ladd to blame for this?

YOU'RE KIDDING. ARE YOU SURE?

THEY RAN THE TEST THREE TIMES. IT'S NO MISTAKE.

THEY FOUND IT IN THE RED ICE CREAM, DIDN'T THEY?

YES. PBUTTER TESTED CLEAN. MPD CONTACTED. WORKING WITH US TO LET US BRING IN SONYA

LADD. LET THE HOSPITAL KNOW.

COUNT ON IT, I texted back. Grunting irritably, I put the phone back in my pocket.

"Has he figured out what's going on?" a weak voice asked.

Sighing, I looked at Jillian. She was awake and was watching me closely.

"I'm sorry for waking you. How did you know I was texting Vance?"

"Because I know *you*. And, I heard your breathing change, like something had just angered you. Knowing you as well as I do, you're going to want to get to the bottom of this, and I have to confess, I'd like to know what happened, too."

I leaned over and pressed the button on the inside of her bed that signaled the nurse.

"Mrs. Anderson?" a female voice asked, from a speaker. "What can I help you with?"

"Zack here," I announced. "I have an update on what she ended up ingesting. You guys are going to want to hear this."

"We're on our way," the nurse assured me.

Less than thirty seconds later, two nurses and one doctor were standing in the room.

I took a deep breath. "Somehow, fentanyl found its way into that ice cream."

Jillian gasped and leveled a stern look at me. "Zachary, are you sure? That's a serious allegation."

"Vance's team checked three times. The red ice cream had fentanyl in it."

The doctor nodded, turned to his nurses, and began issuing orders. More blood was taken, and from the snippets of the conversation I could follow, some drug called naloxone was pulled and prepped for administration.

"There has to be an explanation," Jillian insisted. "I know she wouldn't do this willingly."

"The PVPD has teamed up with Medford. They're working on bringing her in. I think PV is going to try and get her brought here, and not to MPD."

"Why would MPD do that knowing there's a wager at stake?" Jillian asked.

I sobered. "You're right. They wouldn't. Son of a gun. They're planning on getting to her first, to see about …"

My phone buzzed, causing me to jump. "I'm sorry. Let me just send this to voice mail. They can … it's Vance."

"You'd better take it outside."

I gave her a tender kiss and hurried outside.

"What's up, pal?"

"I'm sorry to bother you," Vance began. "I hope you didn't get into trouble for answering your phone at a hospital."

"I'm way ahead of you. I'm standing outside. What's up? Are you going to tell me that Medford brought her in, but have no intention of letting us interrogate her?"

"The warrant is waiting to be signed by a judge," Vance told me. "And MPD says they're more than willing to share their witness with us. However, you're right. They're planning on talking to her first. Wait, forget about that for now. You're never going to believe what happened."

"Hit me with your best. What's up?"

"There's been a third robbery!"

TEN

This time, the robbery was located in southern Medford, which meant Vance and I wouldn't be allowed to check out the crime scene until the Medford police were absolutely certain there was nothing more to be learned. That meant we weren't given clearance until early the next day. Personally, that was fine with me. It freed up time for me to spend with Jillian after I took her home from the hospital. She kept telling me she was fine, but I could see in her eyes that she was still in some discomfort. I haven't been able to bring myself to ask how it felt to get your stomach pumped. I only knew it was something I was sincerely hoping I'd never experience.

So, it was the following morning, and Jillian was, thankfully, feeling much better. She was still following doctor's orders by trying to stay off her feet and just rest, but I knew it was going to be difficult. My wife was not accustomed to having things done for her, and to have to constantly ask for help was a struggle. Therefore, I made myself available twenty-four seven. If she needed a glass of water, or a snack, or even a break from the dogs, then I was there to make sure it happened.

As for Sherlock and Watson, they knew something was up with Jillian. Both of them hovered over her, choosing to flat-out ignore me and snuggle with her instead. I couldn't get angry over that. There was the woman I loved, stretched out on the couch with a light blanket over her, watching television. Stretched out on her right was Sherlock, who had assigned himself guard duties. Watson was on her left, snoozing away.

I was surprised Vance hadn't called by now. After all, the third robbery had happened yesterday afternoon. He promised me he'd let me know as soon as he was cleared to check out the crime scene. However, I also know Medford would make pretty darn certain they hadn't missed anything before releasing the scene to us, so they were probably taking their sweet time.

The text came a few minutes before ten. Medford police had crawled over every square inch of the burglarized store and were satisfied they had looked under every pebble, so to speak. Therefore, they didn't care who wanted to look at their *leftovers*. Well, Vance told me he was already on his way and was hoping I'd be able to meet him there.

"Go," Jillian urged. "I'm fine, Zachary. Really, I am."

Another text message was sent out. Confused, Jillian pointed at my phone.

"Did you just send a text to someone?"

"Hopefully, my replacement. I'm not about to … there we go. She said she can do it."

"Who?" my wife asked.

"Dottie. I asked her to come over here to just sit with you, in case you needed anything. I'm not leaving here until I know someone will be keeping an eye on you."

"I'm not an invalid. I can take care of myself, you know."

"Not after that ordeal, you're not," I argued. "Perfect. She let me know she's on her way."

Jillian sighed. "Thank you. Just do me a favor. Don't keep Vance waiting. Take the dogs and get going. Dottie's house is less than ten minutes from us. I promise to send a text as soon as she's here."

I looked at the dogs, who were watching me intently. "That'll work. Sherlock? Watson? Let's go see if we can catch the person who did this to her, okay?"

Both corgis leapt from the couch and ran to the door.

"Be safe, Zachary," my wife called. "Please keep me posted."

"I promise," I said, as I gave her a kiss. "If I don't get a text from you in the next ten minutes or so, rest assured, I'll be flipping a b—, um, er, I'll be turning around."

Once we were on the road, my GPS informed me we were twelve minutes away from Chunky Slice of Heaven. Located off of Center Avenue, which is only a hop, skip, and a jump away from Harry and

David's country village store, I parked my Jeep next to Vance's sedan. The dogs had just been placed on the ground when my phone chirped, signaling an incoming text message: Dottie had arrived.

Once the leashes were clipped on, the dogs and I headed for the door, only I had a frown on my face before I made it inside. And, I will say that my scowl matched Vance's. Why were we angry? Well, for starters, the store was back open for business, and actually had customers waiting in line!

"What's the deal?" I asked, as soon as we entered. "I thought this was a crime scene. We probably shouldn't be in here, not when they're open and selling ice cream."

Before my detective friend could answer, one of the three people behind the counter noticed us, smiled, and headed toward us. She was tall, thin, and wore her brunette hair long.

"You don't look like paying customers," the woman observed. "Would you be with the police?"

Vance flashed his badge. "Detective Samuelson, PVPD. Can I assume you've had a flood of cops run through here?"

The woman nodded. "Like you wouldn't believe. So upsetting. I've run businesses all across the Pacific Northwest. This is the first time I've ever had someone break in to one of my stores. Excuse me, where are my manners? I'm Janice Peters. And you are?"

"Zack Anderson," I said, offering the owner a smile. I shook her hand. "And down there are

Sherlock and Watson. We were hoping to ..."

"I'm sorry," Janice interrupted, holding up her hands in a *wait* gesture. "Just a moment. Did you say your dogs' names are Sherlock and Watson? Next, you'll tell me you were married in England."

I grinned and gave her a tiny shrug. "Maybe."

"I saw the video online! You were married in Westminster!"

That comment got a few people in line to turn around. "Maybe."

Vance appeared at my side and slapped my back. "Yep, this is him. He even met the Queen of England. She was a huge fan of these dogs."

"Thanks, pal," I muttered. I may have sounded angry, but I was still smiling.

That's when I realized why Vance had made that announcement. Suddenly, there was no one standing in line. Everyone was crowding around us and taking pictures of the dogs. In the meantime, Vance casually approached the counter and began asking questions. I, too, was asked questions, but it had nothing to do with the case.

"Are they really that smart?"

"What do you feed them?"

"Did you really meet Queen Elizabeth II?"

"When did you figure out your dogs were smarter than everyone else?"

On and on it went. I finally had to put my hands up in a time-out gesture. "Guys? We're here because of what happened yesterday. You're fans of the dogs? Perhaps you could help us. What have you heard about the robbery that took place here yesterday afternoon?"

"I heard it was a gang," one person said.

"Nothing doing. It was one guy, and I heard he was wearing a ski mask."

"No, he wasn't," a third piped up. "And there were three of them."

"Was anyone actually here when it happened?" I asked, looking at the dogs' crowd of admirers.

A young guy in his twenties raised his hand. He was holding some type of card in his hand. "I stopped by for a vanilla malt. They're so good, I'm back again today. But, it might have something to do with my card. One more stamp and I get a free one."

"What did you see?" I asked. "Did you notice the guy who did it?"

"Like I said, there were three. They were small, much shorter than me. I was sitting over there, next to the water fountain. I was watching them make my malt, and wondering if they were going to put in the extra scoop of malt that I paid for, when the three of them pushed a couple out of the way and insinuated they were all armed. They were each wearing hoodies, and their backs were to me. I didn't see much of their faces."

"Sunglasses," Janice added. "All three were wearing large sunglasses and black masks, which covered their mouths and the tips of their noses."

"And, I'm guessing you told that to the first set of cops that went through here?"

The owner nodded. "I did."

Overhearing our conversation, Vance wandered over.

"Get anything?" I asked.

"Just what I heard Ms. Peters say, namely that the perps wore dark clothing and hid their faces."

"Are there cameras in here?" I asked, automatically looking up, at the ceiling.

"No, there aren't," Janice reported, sadly shaking her head. "Not yet, that is. I think I'm going to bite the bullet and just order a security system. Better safe than sorry."

"It's a smart move, Ms. Peters," Vance told her. "Do you have any objections to Zack and the dogs looking around? I heard you say you were familiar with their exploits. You do know how they work?"

"I do," Janice confirmed, "and please, help yourself. Ladies and gentlemen, if you're ready to order, please step up to the counter."

Our admirers lost interest and returned to the displays.

Once more, I'm sorry to say that the dogs and I couldn't find diddly squat. We walked the entire grounds of the store, front and back, and didn't find a thing. We opened cabinets, we stopped at the blast chiller, and we even took a walk around the perimeter of the store, just to see if there was anything worth seeing. As far as the dogs were concerned, that was a resounding no. I was about to chalk this robbery up as a freak coincidence when ...

Woof.

I was in the process of returning to my Jeep, so I could secure the dogs inside, when all three of us hesitated. I looked at Sherlock, but he was looking inside the store. Through the windows, I could see Vance, still chatting with Janice Peters. Two female employees were manning the counters, and there were probably five or six customers inside. What, then, had attracted Sherlock's attention?

"Come on, guys. I think this warrants a second look. Sherlock? Lead the way, pal."

Once inside, I gave Sherlock some extra slack in his leash and watched him approach the display counters. In this case, there were three of them. Each display consisted of a left segment, and a right, each holding six tubs. That meant there were thirty-six different flavors in this store. Surely, the earlier investigators did their due diligence and checked them all out? What, then, was Sherlock woofing about?

My tri-colored boy approached the first case and sniffed along the base of it. Not wanting to be left out, Watson headed for the second. Each of them sniffed along the floor, moving from left to right. Sherlock then moved to the second, while Watson headed for the third. Sherlock didn't find anything on the second, either, but I couldn't help notice that Watson had stopped on the right half of the third cabinet. A few moments later, Sherlock joined her. They briefly sniffed noses before sitting and turning to look at me.

"What'd they find?" Vance eagerly asked. "This is good, right?"

"Something caught their attention," I said, nodding. "I just don't know what. What do you see, guys? Or, better yet, what do you smell?"

"What's going on?" Janice asked.

Vance pointed at the third case.

"You mentioned to me just a little bit ago that you reported two tubs of ice cream stolen. By any chance, were they in this case?"

Much to my surprise, Janice shook her head. "As a matter of fact, both were in the first, on your left."

Vance wandered back to the first case to take a look. I tried to follow, only the corgis weren't having any part of it. Sherlock looked as though he was ready to start howling at me, while Watson whined.

"What's the deal, guys? What's with this one? Fine, fine. Look. I'm taking a picture. In fact, I took two. Are you happy now?"

Mollified, both dogs gave themselves a shake and headed for the door. Several onlookers laughed at their antics as I took them outside.

"What's so special about the third case?" Vance wanted to know, once he followed me outside several minutes later.

"Beats me. That's where they have other offerings besides ice cream: gelato, sorbet, and sherbet. As is the norm with the dogs, I took a picture and they lost interest."

"We should be getting close to our pizza party," Vance said, as he helped me load the dogs into my car. "Tomorrow is Friday. Are you ready to go over the pictures?"

For those keeping track of what pictures I've taken on behalf of the dogs, once enough photographs have been taken, then I'll typically gather all of our friends together at a restaurant of my choosing—since I'm the one picking up the tab—and review everything that has caught the dogs' attention. My hope is that, one day soon, we'll be able to interpret the pictures and figure out why they're relevant to the case. However, with as many cases that we have under our belt, the humans have yet to solve the case before the dogs.

"Yeah, I think …"

I was cut off as Vance's cell rang. He stepped away from my Jeep and headed for his sedan. But, after only a few steps, my friend stopped dead in his tracks. He quickly motioned me over as he tapped the speaker button on his phone.

"Say that again, would you?"

"Which part?" a female voice asked.

"All of it, please."

"Very well. Detective Samuelson, this is Marjorie Wallace, from Rascal Valley Labs. As you have requested, we tested the two samples of ice cream you've submitted from your case. I was calling to inform you that, as you surmised, not all were tainted. The first we tested was Gone Nutty, and it was clean."

"Go on," Vance urged. "Tell me the other part."

"What's going on?" I whispered.

Vance held a finger to his lips.

"The results from the second flavor," Marjorie continued, "Red Dawn, matched yours: positive for fentanyl. We have since identified the source of the fentanyl. It was the carob sprinkles. They are, in fact, *not* carob, but candy-coated fentanyl pieces."

"The sprinkles," I breathed, thinking hard. I knew several of the other ice creams had sprinkles in them. But, had any of them contained what should have been carob?

"Thanks, Marjorie. I hope to have more samples for you shortly."

"We stand ready to assist," came Marjorie's polite response, as she terminated the call.

"To answer your question, Zack, no. There are none."

"You couldn't possibly know what I'm thinking."

"You're wondering if any of the other flavors had carob sprinkles in them. The answer is no, they don't."

"Color me impressed," I said, turning to look at my Jeep. Both corgis had their noses squished against the passenger window as they watched me. "All right, if she didn't sell any other tubs with those carob sprinkles, then the question I have is, did she use those sprinkles in anything else? She's already shown us she doesn't limit herself to just ice cream."

"Damn, buddy. That's a good question."

"Can we go find out? She's only about ten minutes away from us."

"Medford PD already picked her up," Vance said, with a sigh. "There's no way to confirm that until we get a chance to talk to her."

"By that time, the MPD will probably have solved the case," I groaned. "What can we do? It's not like we can get Sonya to tell us if she used those sprinkles in anything else."

"Those sprinkles," Vance repeated. With a curse, he whipped out his notebook and began flipping through the pages. After a few moments, he looked up at me with a triumphant expression. "I think that's it, Zack! The other ice cream, the tubs that were reported stolen, they had sprinkles in them. Think about it. If people were trying to hide the fentanyl inside carob sprinkles, then …"

"… what's to prevent them from hiding them in *other* types of sprinkles?" I finished.

"Exactly! Look. Remember Morning Buzz? It had mocha sprinkles. And the original tub of ice cream that was stolen from Jillian? It was called Hawaiian Sunrise. It had—wait for it—toasted coconut sprinkles in it."

"We need to confirm this," I said, growing excited. "But, the question is, how?"

"I say we go back to Corner Delights," Vance suggested. "Vino's place. Maybe, just maybe, there's something there we missed? Maybe he used the ice cream to make a cake? Or a specialty dessert?"

I looked at my friend and gave him a thumbs up. "Get going! I'll be right behind you."

Well, it was a good idea. However, we weren't the only ones who came up with it. By the time we pulled into Corner Delights, three of Medford's finest were also arriving. The officers ignored us until I pulled out Sherlock and Watson.

"The detective dogs," one of the officers said, giving us a smile. "They're Sherlock and Watson, aren't they?"

I made the introductions, in which both corgis greeted the three officers. The one who greeted us first, Officer Arronson, according to the embroidered name on his uniform, squatted next to the dogs and gave them a few friendly scratches. The policeman was in his late twenties, taller than me, and in much better shape, I'm sorry to say. But, I could see he liked dogs. I had to stop the corgis from rolling onto their backs in the middle of the asphalt parking lot.

Two female officers approached next. Both leaned forward to hold out their hands. The younger one, with her blond hair pulled up into a bun, smiled warmly at the dogs. She faced the two of us and held out a hand. "Officer Teri Henderson, Medford PD."

The second female approached and did the same. This one, I noticed, was not wearing a standard police uniform but a blue blouse, black slacks, and a gray overcoat. "Detective Amanda Cartez. You're Detective Samuelson?"

I pointed at Vance. "He is. The only role I have is to hold on to their leashes, I guess."

Detective Cartez looked down at the dogs and nodded. "Those two I know, which means I know you, too, Mr. Anderson. It's a pleasure. Can I ask what you two are doing here?"

"Probably the same as you," Vance stated. "We just received word that fentanyl was found in carob sprinkles. Unfortunately, they were consumed by a civilian, and ..."

Both women gasped.

"This woman, she's okay?" Detective Cartez asked.

I held up a hand. "She will be. She's my wife."

"I'm so tired of these drug traffickers," Detective Cartez scowled. She turned to me and offered me a smile. "Every time I think I've seen it all, I'm consistently proven wrong. They hid drugs in what should be harmless dessert sprinkles. At least in this case I can say that I'm very glad to hear your wife will make a full recovery. Rest assured, we are going to get to the bottom of this."

"Not if we get there first," Vance quipped.

I held my breath. It wasn't something I would have personally said, seeing how I haven't known these people long enough to make a joke like that. Fortunately, Detective Cartez smiled and nodded.

"I am aware of the wager between our departments. That's why the three of us are here.

We want to see if Mr. Gasbardi has used his Morning Buzz flavor in any of his other desserts. We suspect the fentanyl might be hiding in other flavored sprinkles, too."

"That's exactly why we're here," Vance finally admitted. He offered the Medford detective his own smile. "When it comes to something as dangerous as that drug, I personally don't care who wins the wager. I want the person responsible for putting it on the street to pay."

Detective Cartez nodded. "My point exactly. Shall we?"

The five of us, plus two dogs, entered the store. We were in luck. Vino Gasbardi was currently the person manning the counter.

"Detective Samuelson! Mr. Anderson! Welcome back! And it looks like you brought some friends."

Introductions were made. Surprisingly, Amanda nodded in Vance's direction, giving him permission to approach.

"Morning Buzz. You remember it, right?"

The shop owner nodded. "I do. What of it? I have none left, I'm sorry to say."

Vance pointed at the case with a selection of ice cream sandwiches, decorated cones, cakes, and pies. "Did you use it in any other desserts?"

Vino fell silent as he turned to look at the display. "Let me think. I'd have to say no, but I will also say that, if I did, then it'd be gone. Everything in that display was ruined when we were hit. My nephews had a terrible time cleaning out that mess. So, no, there wouldn't be ... wait."

I noticed both Vance and the Medford detective jerked their heads up at the same time, in the same manner.

"The mess," Vino said. "Everything was melted or destroyed. It was thrown away."

"And ...?" Detective Cartez prompted.

Vince hooked a thumb behind him. "The dumpster is back there. I know for a fact that the trash hasn't come yet. It means it's still back there."

A look of gratitude appeared on Amanda's face. "That's wonderful news, Mr. Gasbardi. Officer Arronson, Officer Henderson, you know what I'm going to say, don't you?"

Both cops nodded. "Yes, ma'am," Arronson said. "Retrieve the trash. We're on it."

Once the two officers had left, Amanda gave the two dogs a brief scratch behind the ears.

"I had better keep an eye on them. Detective—er, Vance— I wanted to let you know that, well, if I find anything out, I will let you know regardless of the outcome of our wager."

Vance held out a hand. "Ditto."

I tapped my friend on the shoulder. "Should we go out there and help them?"

"We'd just be in the way," Vance said, shaking his head. "And personally, I'd rather not smell like garbage. I'll wear the billboard and parade around town if necessary."

I turned to Vino. "Thanks for the help. I'm really hoping it'll ... what?"

Vino had crossed his arms over his chest and had a very smug expression on his face.

"Hang on a second, would you?"

Vance shrugged. "Okay. Have you thought of anything else?"

Vino shook his head and held up a finger, signaling us to wait. We waited, in silence, for a few minutes. Finally, the Medford cops reappeared, holding several trash bags. They waved to us, loaded their haul into one unlucky squad car, and drove off.

"I really want to see Pomme Valley win this bet of yours," Vino said. "So, with that said, I have something for you."

He retreated to the back room. When he returned, he was holding a hand-packed pint of ice cream. "Here. It's my own stash of Morning Buzz. My wife is a coffee fanatic, and I was going to surprise her with it on her birthday in just a few days. Now that I've heard that it could be laced with dangerous drugs, I want nothing to do with it. You take it."

We thanked the owner and practically ran to our cars. As soon as we were on the road, I called Vance. "What now?" I asked. "How fast does it take to test something for the presence of illegal drugs?"

"Almost instantaneous," Vance answered. "We have started carrying a selection of instant drug tests, which will indicate the presence of certain chemicals. We take a sample, add it to a solution, and if it turns a specific color, presto! We have our results. One of those tests, I happen to know, looks for fentanyl."

Half an hour later, the four of us, including the dogs, were in Vance's small office. Sherlock and Watson, disinterested in what we were doing, stretched out on the floor while Vance dug out a sample of ice cream with a plastic spoon he pulled from within his desk.

"Okay, I've got my test strips here," Vance was saying. "You'll have to bear with me. I haven't ever used these before. Now, it says we take a supply of the drug and dissolve it in water."

I snatched a half-full bottle that was on the corner of Vance's desk. "Will this do?"

"We need something smaller than that to mix it in. Grab a cup from the water cooler, would you? It's just around the corner."

"Will do."

Once we had the cup, Vance added several tablespoons of water before mixing in the spoonful of ice cream.

"Whoa, dude. You've got too much water in there."

Vance shook his head. "It says here that these strips are super sensitive. If there's fentanyl in here, then this strip will let us know. Good. Now, we dip the strip into the liquid for fifteen seconds. Then, we put it on a flat surface and we wait."

I watched Vance lay the strip of paper on his desk.

"How long do we wait?"

"At least five minutes."

The captain appeared. "Samuelson, there you are. Where the hell have you ... what's that? Is that a fentanyl test strip?"

Vance nodded. He pointed at the pint of ice cream. "If this strip gives us the result we think it will, then you should take possession of that."

Captain Nelson stared at the small container. "Is this from that Sonya Ladd woman?"

"Kinda," I answered. "It's actually from Vino Gasbardi's store. The container is Morning Buzz, which is one of Sonya Ladd's flavors. This one is supposed to have mocha sprinkles. We think those sprinkles ..."

"... are fentanyl," the captain interrupted. "How long before you know?"

"When we know, you'll know," Vance promised.

The captain stared at the strip for a few moments before nodding. Then, he was gone.

"That went over better than I expected," Vance admitted, letting out the breath he had been holding.

"It's going to go over exceptionally well if we get a positive hit," I said.

The gods must have been smiling at us. Five minutes later, we were looking at two lines on the fentanyl test strip. Our theory had been confirmed! The sprinkles contained a very illegal drug. That was why those stores had been burglarized. Someone knew what the sprinkles were, and wanted to … wait. That wasn't right. Why take the other flavors if they knew the sprinkles were what they wanted? It almost suggested the opposite, that they didn't know what they were looking for, only that it lay somewhere within the ice cream.

That was why the desserts I saw earlier had been torn apart. The drugs were inside the ice cream, all right, only not in the traditional sense. Whoever was sent to retrieve the drugs hadn't been told how to find them, only that they were in the ice cream.

Vance's desk phone rang.

"Detective Samuelson. Detective Cartez, it's a pleasure. How did you get my number? Forget about it. What can I do for you? Wait, slow down. *Who* found *what* at Sonya Ladd's house? I'll be damned. That's definitely good to know. As long as you're on the phone, I was going to tell you that we came across someone who had a pint of Morning Buzz. Thankfully, no one had touched it yet. Yes, that's right. We ran a test on it. Obviously, you already know the results. So, what now? This isn't looking good for Sonya Ladd, is it?"

Vance motioned for me to close the door to his office. Then, he hit the speaker button on his phone.

"She's been charged with illegal possession of drugs, with the intent to distribute," Detective Amanda Cartez was saying. "However, she still maintains her innocence. Right now, everyone here is trying to find the missing link between

Ladd and the Hansen brothers. Our captain insists the link is there. We just have to find it."

"Good luck, detective," Vance said. "I wish you the best, and I sure hope you find it."

"Thank you, Detective Samuelson."

Vance looked at me. "Am I the only one who thinks we're missing something here? This doesn't add up. We've already looked into Sonya Ladd. She doesn't have any ties with either of the Hansens. I'm starting to think there are more people involved in this scheme than we thought."

"Couldn't agree more, pal. I'm dying to know something. I heard you ask what was found at Sonya Ladd's house. Can you tell me?"

"Two bottles of sprinkles in Sonya's cabinets: one was rainbow, the other solid blue."

"They both tested positive for fentanyl, didn't they?"

"Yes."

"Wow. Okay, you know what? You're right."

"About what?" Vance wanted to know.

"What you said earlier. About our get-together. I think it's time we call in the gang and go over these clues. I honestly believe if we want to solve this case, and I mean tie up *all* loose ends, then we need to figure out what Sherlock and Watson have been trying to tell us. And, I can't believe I'm saying this, I think I'm tired of pizza."

ELEVEN

T here's something I've been meaning to ask you," Vance told me, nearly four hours later. Jillian and I had just arrived for our corgi clue review session and we were in the process of pulling out the chairs next to Vance and Tori.

"What's that?" I asked.

"Earlier, you said something that got me thinking. It was about tying up loose ends. All loose ends. What did you mean by that?"

Nodding, I took the menu Jillian offered me and flipped it open. "It's something we noticed when we were in Alaska. Up there, we were having dinner at a place known for their crab, and …"

"There's a shocker," Vance interrupted, chuckling.

"Right? You'll never find me turning down a free crab dinner, that's for sure. Anyway, we were having dinner and going through the pictures I had taken. Everything had been sorted out, except for one clue. When we realized we had no idea how it fit into the case we were working on, we all delved deeper and found the connection. Man alive, am I glad we checked it out. So, as obscure as these clues are, we need to be darn certain we figure out how everything fits. Every little bit counts."

Vance nodded. "Gotcha."

I looked around the table. Joining us this evening was our usual gang of friends. Vance and his wife, Tori, were on my left. Sitting across from them were Harry Watt and his wife Julie. On the other side of Tori was Dottie.

The waitress came by and took our drink order. After telling her we were going to need a few more minutes before we'd be ready to place our dinner orders, I glanced at the menu for El Marauder's Grill. One thing I'll say about this restaurant: if you were a vegetarian, then you had no business being here. This place had to have, hands-down, the best barbecue south of Portland. The center of this small eatery has a huge circular pit, with all varieties of meat roasting over open flames. Steaks, burgers, briskets, poultry, you name it, if it could be found walking along the ground, then they were probably grilling it.

Jillian decided on the petite filet mignon, while Vance and Harry both ordered steaks. Tori and Julie both ordered salads, but before I could tease them about their choices, each added grilled meat to the top. As for me, I decided on grilled chicken. What can I say? I've never been much of a steak eater.

"I got a feelin', bro," Harry announced, after taking a sip of his iced tea and looking enviously at my bottle of beer. "Today's the day we prove we're smarter than your dogs."

I noticed Harry eyeing my beer and deliberately took a long swallow. Jillian saw what I was doing and placed her hand over mine, prepared to dig in. Harry smirked, but then Julie thumped him in the gut.

Dottie rubbed her hands together. "So! Where do we start?"

I pulled my phone out and placed it on the table. "Everyone here has been a part of one of these get-togethers, haven't you? Therefore, you should all be in my address book. So, all I have to do is …"

Vance held up a hand. "Would you wait for just a few minutes?"

I paused as I looked at the detective. "Umm, all right. What's the matter?"

Vance checked his watch. "Oh, nothing. I just thought this was the part where we all give updates on our week. I mean, isn't that what we do? Share what's going on in our lives?"

Harry and I stared at our friend as though he had just announced he was signing up to do a repeat performance of his Peter Pan dance number. If you're wondering what that is all about, then I would recommend checking YouTube. Vance made a foolish bet against the dogs a while back and it had blown up in his face in a spectacular fashion.

Jillian and I shared a look and then shrugged.

"You're right, Vance," my wife said. "This is

a time to share what's going on with our lives. We don't need to hear from Vance or Zachary. I mean, we will, but just not yet. So, I'll go first. As you all know, Cookbook Nook had its first robbery. They made a mess of things, but there was no real damage, aside from a broken front door. It's already been replaced and we're open for business."

"I sure do hope they catch them," Julie said. "Not much on our end, aside from Shawn and Andi becoming more mobile every day. It's all we can do to keep up with them. Need to exercise more? Want to lose some weight? Have twins. You'll kiss your free time goodbye."

"And sleep," Harry added. "I haven't slept more than three hours straight since they were born, man."

"But, your kids are healthy," Tori said. "You all have your health. That's what you need to be thankful for."

Harry's face lit up. "Oh! I totally forgot to tell you guys! I finally found another vet. He starts in a few weeks and will help cover weekends and after-hour emergencies. I figured I already have enough on my plate. Getting woken up at three in the morning by your phone is the worst, man."

"Good for you, pal," I said. "Your clinic is always busy. Glad to hear you're getting some help. Although, I thought you already did?"

"I did hire someone a few months ago," Harry said, nodding. "He didn't last, man. Thought it'd be a cush job and he would have a say in how I ran things. Should've seen the look on his face when I said otherwise. Complained like crazy, bro."

"What about you, Tori?" Jillian asked, turning to her friend. "Did anything fun and exciting happen to you?"

Vance's red-headed wife smiled. "Ballroom dancing."

Jillian blinked a few times. "You went ballroom dancing? How fun!"

"No, I'm thinking about starting a class at the rec center. I've had a couple of people ask if I could teach them to waltz, or the cha-cha, and even the tango. I told them I knew the dances, but had never taught anyone them. But, if I get enough people interested, I would." Tori deliberately pointed at each of us as she counted. "Well, there's one, two, three, four, Vance is five, I'm six, and Dottie is seven. Add the three who asked, and you know what? I'm thinking I have my class!"

I thought about opening my mouth to protest, but I knew there was no need. I heard Harry start sputtering and knew he had the bases covered.

"Ballroom dancing? Like, you think I want to learn how to do the tango? I'm not a dancer, man, so I got one thing to say about that."

Tori batted her eyes at Harry. "And what would that be?"

"That I'd love to learn," Harry quickly answered. I noticed Julie's hands had dropped below the table, so I presume she was employing the same trick Jillian used on me and had dug her nails into Harry's flesh. "That's me, one loving and supporting hubby."

Julie blew him a kiss before returning both hands to the top of the table. Jillian looked at me with a hopeful expression. "Sure, why not? Dottie? Are you in?"

"I don't have a partner," the girl lamented. "I don't want to take dancing classes by myself."

Jillian nodded. "I can understand that. We won't force you to come, but I do hope you can find a partner. We'd love to include you with us."

"I'll find someone," Dottie vowed. "Is it my turn? I've been waiting so long to make this announcement, and now, I finally can! A Lazy Afternoon is turning a profit!"

"I personally liked you announcing *you're black* to the world," I said, giving our group's youngest member a friendly smile.

Dottie blushed. "That is soooo not what I meant."

I picked up my phone and created a shared folder. While I sent out electronic invitations, I asked Vance to fill everyone in on the case. Once heads were nodding, and a few questions had been asked, I held up my phone and waited for everyone to do the same.

"Okay, I can see everyone has joined. So, why don't we …"

Vance held up a hand. "Wait a minute."

"What's with you?" I asked, as I turned to

my friend. "Why do I get the impression you're stalling for time? What are you waiting for?"

"Me. I'm sorry I'm late."

The table fell silent as we turned to the newcomer. Vance rose to his feet. "Detective Cartez. I'm glad you could join us."

"I don't think I've ever been here before," Amanda said, as she pulled out a chair next to Dottie.

"Then you have no idea what you've been missing," I said, grinning. "If you're vegan, or a vegetarian, then be prepared to be lured to the dark side. If you're not, welcome to your new favorite restaurant. I'm not a steak eater, but this place would definitely make one out of me."

Introductions were made, and the Medford detective placed her drink and food orders.

"Before we get started," Vance began, "can I ask if there've been any developments?"

Amanda sighed. "You could say that, I suppose. Sonya Ladd claims she has an alibi for the time of both Hansen murders."

I let out a breath and sat back in my chair. "I knew she couldn't have been the one behind all of this. Well? What's her alibi?"

Amanda nodded. "Ms. Ladd claims she was in Sacramento for a few days, on a college scouting trip. Her son graduates this year, and she's determined to see him enrolled for the fall semester."

"I'll bet your captain loved hearing that," Vance

said.

Amanda scowled. "It didn't go over well. I've reached out to both universities and the hotel she stayed at, looking for confirmation she was there. What about you people?"

"Nothing new since we spoke last," Vance reported. "That's why you're here. We're going to be working on the case, and in the spirit of full disclosure, I thought someone from Medford might like to sit in with us."

"Thank you for inviting me. Did I understand you correctly on the phone? You're all going to review a number of clues? What clues are these, and how come I don't know about them?"

"Corgi clues," I corrected. "It's nothing official, but the dogs have yet to be wrong. You remember us telling you how the corgis worked? Well, we've learned long ago that the more eyes we have deciphering these *clues*, the better. And, thanks to the advances of modern technology, if you have an Apple iPhone, I can invite you to see a shared album, so you'll be looking at everything we have."

Amanda held up a large, glossy smart phone. "I don't, I'm sorry to say. This is a Google phone."

I shrugged. "No one's perfect. Dottie? Would you be willing to share with her?"

Dottie nodded. "Of course. Detective Cartez, scooch a little closer, would you?"

"Call me Amanda. Alright, let's see how this is done."

I nodded. "You got it. Now, first up, everyone

should be looking at the first picture in the folder. What you're looking at is a photo taken inside Cookbook Nook." I saw Detective Cartez give me a blank expression. "Oh, uh, that'd be Jillian's store. It was the first place to be robbed."

Amanda nodded. "Ice cream. Your store sells ice cream?"

"Well, it's a kitchen store, as the name suggests," Jillian explained. "On the second floor, I have a little café, and we just recently started selling ice cream."

"Got it. So, what am I looking at?"

"This is a picture taken near Jillian's Decorations section in her vast collection of cookbooks. We're thinking the clue is the rainbow."

"How do you know the clue isn't supposed to be grass?" Amanda asked. "Or meadow? Or what about green? What about outdoors?"

The seven of us gave our new friend knowing smiles.

"Oh, you'll see," I promised. "Anyway, this was the day we returned from Alaska. We were home only long enough to drop our stuff and grab a car."

"Rainbows," Amanda repeated. "Should I be writing this down?"

Vance held up his notebook. "It's not a bad idea. I already have everything in mine."

Amanda pulled a similar-sized notebook from her purse. Within moments, I saw her jot a few notes. In shorthand, I might add.

"Showoff," Vance muttered, once he caught a

look at her notes. Tori then punched him on the arm.

"Okay, next up we have not one, nor two, but three pictures of kids. For those of you who think I'm being creepy ..."

Vance and Harry immediately raised their hands.

"... you can bite me. For these pictures, I'm under the impression we should be focusing on the backpacks."

"How do you know?" Amanda asked.

"Because of Sherlock and Watson," I answered. "We saw kids of all shapes and sizes. Same for the backpacks. The corgis ignored most, but focused on the ones visible in the photographs. Now, here's the kicker. It could be a specific kid, or style of backpack, or even a color, I guess. I just don't know which."

"Then, all we're doing is theorizing," Amanda said, letting out a sigh.

"We need to get through all the pictures first," Jillian said. "Then, after we've seen everything, we can try to brainstorm some ideas in which the clues could be relevant to the case. I'll also point out that this isn't the only backpack clue."

"Kids and backpacks," Amanda said aloud, as she wrote in her notebook. "What are the circumstances of the pictures?"

"They were taken inside Cookbook Nook," Jillian reported. "I remember this. It was a school outing. A teacher was rewarding her pupils for not missing any class."

More writing.

"Anyone have any comments?" I asked the table.

Harry opened his wallet and slapped something on the table. "I got twenty bucks that says there's no way rainbows are involved in this case."

I pointed at Harry's hand, which was resting on top of the bill he had placed. "I'll treat this as a chess move. You haven't moved your hand yet, so you have the chance to take back your oh-so-foolish gesture. Are you sure you want to make that bet?"

A look of doubt crossed Harry's features. After a few moments, he shrugged. "Sherlock and Watson can't be right all the time. Yeah, the bet stands. No rainbows."

I pulled out a twenty. "I'll see that bet."

Twenty-dollar bills appeared out of thin air.

"I'm in," Vance said.

"Me, too," said Dottie.

Tori dug into her purse the same time Jillian opened her wallet.

"Count me in," my wife announced.

"Ditto," added Tori.

In silence, we turned to Amanda. "If I could raise, I would. My instinct is saying I should trust your dogs. I'm in."

I gave a small cough. "Okay, before Harry loses any more money, or what's left of his dignity, let's move on. Oh, hey, Vance? Would you like to describe this next one?"

"Bite me, buddy."

"That was rude," Tori scolded, as she gave Vance a frown. "What was that for?"

"Look at the picture first," I suggested.

Tori looked at her phone, studied the image, and then shrugged.

"What am I looking at? The inside of someone's house?"

"This is the dead brother's apartment," I said. "We're in Medford now, and the dogs had just looked inside the cabinets under the kitchen sink. Do you see that black blur on the ground? It's a cockroach."

"Oh, ewww!" Dottie exclaimed.

"I'm with you," Amanda said, shuddering. "I hate roaches."

"Well, so does Vance," I said, suppressing a laugh. "He …"

"Oh, do we have to do this now?" Vance complained.

Tori slapped a hand over her mouth. "I know how you are with bugs, dear. What did you do?" When Vance refrained from answering, Tori looked at me. "What did he do?"

"Let's just say that the average human male is not able to scale walls, like a spider. However, poor Vance tried anyway."

There was a round of laughter at the table.

"You poor thing," Jillian said. "I think I'd

probably faint dead away if something like that came at me."

"It was at least a foot long," Vance confirmed.

"No, it wasn't," I argued, laughing.

"Close enough."

"Wait," Amanda said, holding up a hand. "This is a clue? This cockroach? What does a cockroach have to do with anything?"

"And *that* is why we're here," Jillian said.

Amanda nodded. "I see where you're going with this. These clues appear to be nonsense, yet somehow, they're related? How very interesting!"

"No one?" I asked, holding up my phone. "All right, moving to the next. No, wait. We have a picture of Vance sitting on the counter, looking scared. Sorry, pal. I thought I deleted that one."

Vance shook his head and glared at me.

"Right. Okay, we're onto the dumpster shot. Everyone see the tub of ice cream?"

"This isn't the one that was stolen from me, was it?" Jillian asked.

"No, this was outside of the dead brother's apartment," I corrected. "This was taken only a few minutes after Vance screamed like a girl and …"

"Just you wait, buddy," Vance scowled.

"… the corgis pulled me over to the dumpster," I continued, giving Vance a grin. "Once I opened it, I saw the tub."

Jillian's hand grabbed my arm. "Zachary? Do you see that? Zoom in on the plastic container next to the tub."

"Looks like cookies," I observed.

"Zoom in a little more. Look! Do you see what's *on* those cookies?"

"Sprinkles," Amanda said, awed. "You've got to be kidding me. Rainbow sprinkles! Do we know if this is what they wanted you to see?"

I looked over at Vance, who shrugged. "I guess so. I thought it was the ice cream, but for all I know, they were telling us to pay attention to the sprinkles."

"What about the sprinkles?" Harry wanted to know.

"Fentanyl," Amanda said, eliciting gasps from the table. "The sprinkles in several of those flavors of ice cream tested positive for it. I think Zack is right. The dogs are trying to get you to pay attention to the sprinkles."

"That makes sense," I said. "One of these days, I'll figure out how they do it. Harry? Another rainbow clue. Huh. Worried yet? Now, moving on. What's next?"

"I'm looking at a strange man," Tori reported. "Who is this?"

I glanced at the next picture. "Here we have Tommaso, nephew of Vino Gasbardi."

"And is this someone we know?" Harry asked.

"Vino is the owner of the second ice cream shop," Amanda reported. "I knew about the nephews, but I didn't know what they looked like. Why did you take his picture?"

"Because Sherlock and Watson wouldn't stop staring at him," I told the Medford detective. "I figured there was something about him that I needed to see, but I've still yet to see it. The closest I've come is to look at what's hanging from his neck. He's got a pair of sunglasses resting on his chest. Everyone see 'em?"

There was a chorus of affirmative noises.

"Rainbows, kids, sprinkles, and sunglasses," Amanda said, as she hastily scribbled notes. "This is making no sense."

"Welcome to the club," Vance said, grinning.

Amanda finished writing and looked up. "Hey, I'm so lost it's not even funny, and I'm a detective. Whatever. Bring on the next. Whatcha got for us?"

Dottie leaned close and swiped to the next picture.

"Oh, these," I said, as I looked at my phone. "I forgot about them. I don't think they are clues. I took 'em to show the cops once this kid sped off. You're looking at a picture of Barry Foster, owner of the small green truck there. He's the one who purchased the missing tubs of ice cream from Corner Delight, Vino's store."

Tori looked up. "Wait, what? He bought them? I thought it was a robbery!"

"So did we," Vance confirmed. "The store was still trashed, yet the kid's story checks out. He paid for the ice cream, so we couldn't press any charges against him."

"We still don't know who trashed Vino's store,"

I said, as I noticed Harry's mouth open. "I don't know if we'll ever know. We just know it wasn't him. All right, keep scrolling. Looks like I took four pictures of Barry and his truck."

"And now we have more pictures of ice cream," Jillian said, as she studied her phone. "Looks like two tubs that ... oh, wait. I recognize these flavors. Oregon Crostini and Garden Delight. We found them a couple of days ago, when we were driving around the area, right? In the Ruxton?"

Two things happened simultaneously. I saw Harry cringe once he heard the names of the flavors, and at the mention of my roadster, I watched Amanda's head jerk up. "A Ruxton? You have a working, running Ruxton?"

"A 1930 Ruxton Sedan," I confirmed. "It's not a very well-known car. I'm impressed you've heard of it."

"My father is a huge car buff," Amanda explained. "I practically grew up helping him in his garage."

"Sounds like a wonderful childhood," Jillian said.

Amanda nodded and gave my wife an appreciative smile. "Not many people say that. They automatically think I was gypped out of a happy childhood. But, as soon as I argue that I was able to spend practically every waking moment with my father, they usually shut up."

"I'll have to give you and your father a ride in it sometime," I told the Medford detective.

"I'll hold you to that, Mr. Anderson."

"You got it. Now, about these new tubs of ice cream, I'd like to point out that I don't think they're corgi clues. I took them just so that I could show Jillian what I thought were gourmet-flavored ice cream. You know, in case the shop was targeted next. Since it never was, I should've just deleted these, so please ignore them."

"Looks like we have more kids," Tori reported, moving to the next picture. "Was this at another store?"

I looked at Jillian. "This was the third one we hit that day, wasn't it? The one where you refused to get out of the car?"

Jillian giggled. "There were too many people there, even for me."

"Several buses were in the parking lot," I explained to the group. "But, I wanted to check out the store. What do we find? Tons of kids, and if you look at this set of five pictures I took, you'll see that most of the kids are wearing backpacks. That's why I said that we're pretty sure backpacks are involved in some fashion."

Amanda was nodding. "Backpacks. Wait. Let me see something. Dottie, may I?"

Dottie nodded and handed Amanda her phone. The detective swiped left a number of times until the first set of kid pictures was displayed. Studying the photos intensely, Amanda was silent as she flipped back and forth between the sets.

"What do you see?" Vance wanted to know.

"Backpacks," Amanda reported. "Specifically, red ones. If you look at both sets, you'll see that there is a child wearing a red pack in every picture."

Our table fell silent as we studied the photos.

"She's right," Jillian said, after a few minutes had passed. "Red backpacks. What does it mean?"

"That more than likely the person who ultimately responsible for this mess is wearing a backpack," Vance said, although he didn't sound certain. "Maybe? We'll have to see. Whatever happens, that's a great catch, Cartez."

Amanda smiled and nodded. She looked at me and waited for me to continue.

"That's the type of input that we're looking for," I said. "Keep it up, everyone. Now, once you scroll past the pictures of the kids, you're going to find one of a baseball hat. This was when we were in Sonya Ladd's house. I think we were getting ready to leave when the dogs spotted the hat and immediately sat."

"What are we looking at?" Harry asked. "What's on the hat? A celebrity?"

"It's a picture of a famous wrestler," I explained. "He's an actor now. The only common denominator I can think of is …"

"Sunglasses," Amanda interrupted.

I nodded. "Precisely. In the picture, you'll see some sunglasses."

"They're dangling from a holder, just like the Italian guy," Dottie said.

"Tommaso," I confirmed, as I returned to the photo of Vino's nephew. "Sunglasses, and they're dangling around his neck, just like the picture on the hat in Sonya's house. So, the question is, are we still thinking it's sunglasses?"

"What else would it be, bro?" Harry asked.

"It might be the holder," Tori suggested.

I nodded. "That's what I'm thinking. Again, how it relates, I don't know. Sunglass holders. Sherlock and Watson have definitely got us scrambling this time."

"Have we hit the end yet?" Tori asked. "I don't seem to recall having this many pictures before."

"I think they did it on purpose," I said, laughing. "They enjoy showing us who's smarter, and I'm sorry to say, I think it's still them. Let's see. Looks like we have one left. Okay, this is from the last robbery. This is a picture of an entire display full of tubs."

I noticed Jillian zooming in on the picture. "I can save us all some time," my wife announced. "I know why the dogs were looking at this."

"I can't wait to hear this," Amanda said.

Harry held up a hand. "That makes two of us."

"Zoom in on the flavors," Jillian instructed. "And then swipe right, to get to the front flavor furthest to the right. See what it says?"

"I'll be a monkey's uncle," I exclaimed. "Rainbow sherbet."

"Oh, come on," Amanda said, frowning. "There's no way your dogs are that smart."

"They are," Harry and Vance said, at the same time.

"This is impressive on so many levels," Amanda decided. "I don't think Captain Ryerson has a chance of replicating your success."

We all looked up from our phones.

"What was that?" Jillian asked.

My response was a little more than a grunt. "Huh? Whazzat?"

"There's another reason I'm here," Amanda confessed.

Tori nodded. "You're here to see how Sherlock and Watson operate, so that you can let your captain know. From the sound of things, he wants to get a couple of dogs for their department, doesn't he?"

"He's already got them," Amanda clarified, shaking her head. "Past tense. The problem is, the only thing they're good at finding is food. He was hoping I'd be able to see what Sherlock and Watson can do, and then help train Magnus and Seaver to do the same thing."

"Magnus and Seaver?" Vance repeated. "Dare I ask what kinds of dogs those are?"

"Belgian Malinois," Amanda answered. "Talk about your high-strung dogs. I told the captain from the beginning that I didn't think they were going to work out, but Captain Ryerson is persistent—stubborn. He won't give up without a fight."

"What are you gonna tell him about Sherlock

and Watson?" Harry asked.

Amanda shrugged. "The truth. I have absolutely no idea how they're able to identify clues."

"That's the truth, all right," I said, sighing. "Rainbows, backpacks, er, *red* backpacks, cockroaches, and eyeglass holders. Anyone?"

Harry shrugged. "Sounds like we're looking for an assassin who uses a red backpack, wears sunglasses, and maybe has a cockroach tattoo?"

Instead of laughing, like most of us were doing, Amanda was actually nodding. "That's not a bad guess. It fits. You left out the rainbows, though."

Harry frowned. "Oh. Uh, he's gay?"

Julie choked on her drink. "Harrison! That's not okay!"

"It's just a guess, man. Sorry, Jules."

Someone's cell rang, and it sounded like an old-fashioned analog phone. Amanda apologized and started to stand up, intent on taking the call outside. At the exact moment she stood, Vance's phone began to ring, too.

"Tell me that's not a coincidence," I whispered.

Jillian nodded.

"Heading outside?" Vance asked Amanda. "I'll see you out there."

My detective friend answered the phone and followed Amanda to the door. While they were gone, the waitress reappeared and topped off our drinks. Chatter erupted around the table, wondering what news Vance and Amanda were going to give us. Someone turned themselves in? Sonya Ladd changed her story and ended up confessing? Whatever news the two detectives were being given didn't take long. Vance returned first, and had almost made it back to our table when Amanda walked back through the front entrance.

"Everything okay?" I asked.

Vance nodded. "That was Captain Nelson. Cartez? Did you get the same news?"

"Pretty sure I did. Shall I?"

Vance held out an arm. "Please."

"Sonya Ladd's alibis checked out. All three of them. There's no way she is the murderer of the Hansen brothers. Is that what you were told?"

Vance nodded. "Almost verbatim. And the son?"

"What about the son?" Jillian asked.

"Medford is focusing its efforts on locating one Trevor Ladd," Amanda reported.

I looked at Vance. "I thought the kid was clean?"

"He doesn't have a record," Vance confirmed.

"But," Amanda continued, "he has a list of known associates who *do*."

"That doesn't mean he's guilty," Tori protested.

"You didn't hear the best part," Amanda said. "Your dogs? They're totally amazing, by the way. I'm still in shock. Listen, one of Trevor's closest friends is a boy by the name of Jay Raymonds. He's known on the street as ... wait for it ... Skittles."

Harry held up his hands. "So?"

"*Taste the rainbow*," I breathed, as countless childhood commercials flashed before my eyes, spouting that exact slogan.

"Hey, I've heard that before," Harry exclaimed, a few moments later.

Julie sighed. "Harrison, we need to get you out more."

TWELVE

Less than an hour later, Vance and I and the dogs were in one of PVPD's two conference rooms. Also present was Detective Amanda Cartez. I barely had time to kiss Jillian goodbye before I bundled the dogs up and we parted ways at the restaurant. She made me promise to let her know if anything happened.

The Pomme Valley Police Department was quiet. Granted, it wasn't deserted, seeing how there always had to be someone on duty. In this case, it was nearly seven o'clock in the evening, and the two officers on duty gave us a wide berth as we burst into the station and angled straight for conference room one.

"Whatcha got?" a gruff voice asked us, from the doorway.

Looking up, we were surprised to see Captain Nelson entering the room. He slid out a chair next to me and sat down. Then, he noticed Sherlock and Watson staring up at him with hopeful eyes. The captain held out a hand and waited until Vance passed him two doggie biscuits.

"I hear you two managed to pull off another

one. Good job, guys. A very fine job."

"We haven't found Skittles yet," Vance told us. "Er, make that, Jay Raymonds. But, we've got everyone looking for him."

"We've put out word in Medford, too," Detective Cartez announced, which earned her an appreciative nod from the captain.

"What do we know about this Raymonds fellow?" the captain asked.

"He's got a record," Vance began, as he pulled out his notes. "Petty theft, grand theft auto, aggravated assault, and breaking and entering."

"How old is this kid?" I asked.

"Seventeen," Amanda answered.

"Why do they call him Skittles?" Captain Nelson asked.

"Apparently, that's his street name," Vance answered. "I'm told he usually carries around a bag or two. It's his favorite candy."

"A street name suggests he's in a gang," the captain said, stroking his chin. "Look up his known associates. I want to know who he's running with. Find out which one, on the double."

Vance nodded. "Detective Cartez? Would you care to assist?"

"I'd love to," Amanda replied.

The two of them hurried out of the room.

"Your dogs are something else," Captain Nelson told me, as he gave each of them another friendly scratch.

"Did you hear that Medford's captain is trying

to recreate what we've done with Sherlock and Watson?"

The friendly scratching immediately ceased. Two blue-gray eyes were suddenly boring into my own. "Would you run that by me again?"

"Detective Cartez admitted she is tagging along with us with the hopes of being able to report back how Sherlock and Watson discover clues."

"Ryerson wants to get a couple of dogs," Captain Nelson said, shaking his head. "You've always told me that you don't know how your dogs do it."

"True, and that's still the case," I assured him. "And I feel I should point out he already *has* the dogs. Present tense."

Two thick, burly arms were crossed. "Izzat so? Corgis?"

"Belgian Malinois," I corrected.

"That is one hyperactive breed. My nephew has a pair of them. Tell me, Anderson, are they making progress?"

"In training them? From what I hear, absolutely not. And from what Cartez has said, she has no clue how Sherlock and Watson operate, so she doesn't have any info to pass on to the trainers in Medford."

"Good."

The two detectives chose that moment to return. Vance plopped a file down on the table and pointed at it. "The CL Crew."

"The *what*?" I asked, frowning.

"As far as anyone knows, CL refers to Crater

Lake," Vance explained. "They're one of the newest gangs in the state, and as such, I know they'd love to make a reputation for themselves. It says they're heavily recruiting new members."

"So far, they've kept themselves clean," Amanda continued. "Or, they're doing a fantastic job of keeping themselves anonymous. Either way, we found references to some known members, but the only thing we have are their street names."

"And Skittles is one of them," I guessed.

Amanda shook her head. "Actually, no, he isn't. I mean, we know he is, only he's not listed here. That gives you an idea how dated our material is. We have to assume they've set roots in town and their leadership has been established."

"Who's their leader?" the captain wanted to know.

"I don't know," Vance admitted.

"I may be able to shed some light on that," another male voice announced.

Amanda set her phone down on the conference table and slid it closer to us.

Captain Nelson grunted once. "Ryerson. I'd know your voice anywhere. Ready to get your hands dirty?"

"You'd better believe it, Nelson. MPD stands ready to assist."

"You say you can tell us who's heading up CL Crew?"

"The only thing we know about him is that he's a young guy," Captain Ryerson said. "Probably no older than thirty. We've only seen him from a distance. He manages to disappear before anyone can get a good look at him. I've personally seen him twice, and each time, he's wearing a black leather jacket."

"None of the corgi clues are leather jackets, I'm sorry to say," I said.

"What *are* the clues your dogs have found?" Medford's head of police wanted to know.

"Let's see. Red backpacks, eyeglass holders, cockroaches, and rainbows."

"You know how ridiculous that sounds, don't you?" Ryerson asked.

"Over fifteen," Captain Nelson said.

"Over fifteen *what*?" Ryerson asked.

"Over fifteen cases. Murder, theft, missing persons. Those dogs have a better closure rate than anyone I have ever seen. I have no clue how they do it. I know you don't, either, so you might as well give up trying with your Malinois."

"Wh-what? I don't know what you're talking about."

"Your detective does," Nelson insisted. "Listen, let's stop pointing fingers and find these idiots. Samuelson, what's next? Where do we look? Anderson, what do your dogs say?"

I watched Vance open his mouth, but I could tell from his expression he didn't have an answer. Fortunately, I did.

"Trevor Ladd."

Everyone focused on me. "Trevor Ladd," I

555555656567456789101121111

JEFFREY POOLE

repeated. "He's friends with Skittles. Er, Jay Raymonds. We need to talk to him."

Captain Nelson straightened in his chair. He slid a stack of files that were piled next to him over, and began rifling through them. "Why does that name sound familiar."

"I want to know why someone would be called Skittles," Ryerson was heard saying. "Ah, I see. The rainbow connection."

"Exactly. Vance said that CL Crew is recruiting new members. Our link is Trevor Ladd. Bring him in. I say it's time to find out what he knows."

"We'll get working on his location immediately," Ryerson informed us.

"Don't bother," Nelson informed me, as he closed one of the files and looked up. "He was caught speeding in PV city limits with an open container of alcohol. He's presently cooling his jets in a holding tank. That's why the name rang a bell."

"I was wondering where he went," Ryerson said. "We tried picking him up earlier, too, but couldn't locate him at his residence. I believe his mother was ready to tear into him, should she be allowed to do it."

"She's already tried here," Nelson said. "My office is on the other side of the building, with at least half a dozen walls between us, but I could still hear her shouting at him."

"He didn't talk or he didn't want to cooperate?" I asked.

"He refused to cooperate," Nelson answered.

244

"Then, I think our next step is clear," I decided.

I, the one non-police person in the room, was offering a suggestion for what could be done next. Go figure.

"I'm all ears, Anderson," Captain Nelson said.

"Bring him in here," I said. "Plant his butt in one of those chairs. Then, bring his mother in and seat her right next to him. Sonya Ladd doesn't strike me as the type of person who would let her son become tight-lipped, especially if we, that is to say, *you* can offer her son some type of plea arrangement."

Nelson turned to look at Vance. "That's not bad. Not bad at all."

Vance nodded. "Agreed."

Nelson hooked a thumb at the door. "Bring him. And the mother."

"I'll have to see if she's home," Vance began. "She would …"

"She's still here," Nelson insisted. "Trust me."

Captain Nelson knew how to read people, that's for sure. Not only was Sonya waiting in the lobby, she jumped at the chance to see her son and sit in on the interrogation.

"I've got nothing to say to you," Trevor began, as he plopped down in the chair opposite Captain Nelson, Vance, and myself.

I should also point out that this is the first time I've ever participated in an interview while on *this* side of the mirror and not sitting on *that* side of the table.

The door opened and Detective Cartez escorted Sonya in. Trevor's mother took one look at him and immediately frowned. As for Trevor himself, he cringed, and tried to sink down in his seat.

"Would you care to repeat what you just said?" Vance asked, adopting a casual tone.

Trevor cast a nervous look at his mother. "Umm, er, no."

"He said he had nothing to say to us," Vance helpfully supplied.

Sonya turned to look at her son. "You've got five seconds, boy, and five seconds only. Start talking."

"Whadya want to know?" Trevor cried. "That I screwed up? Fine! I admit it!"

"Screwed up *how*?" Sonya asked. Her brow furrowed as she glared at her son, *daring* him to rebel.

"I never should have agreed to hide it."

This was news to us. The captain and both detectives leaned closer.

"What did you hide?" Amanda asked.

Trevor's answer was so faint that I'm surprised we heard it. Then again, it was so quiet in the room that we could've heard a pin drop.

"The sprinkles."

Sonya's eyes widened with disbelief. "That box with all the sprinkles in it. That was you? I thought I was losing my mind! I found it in the pantry and thought … wait. Wait just a moment. Is that what this is all about? What's so important about those sprinkles?"

Vance gave Trevor a pitiful look. "Drugs. Specifically, fentanyl. Whoa, whoa! Put the chair down, Ms. Ladd. I have to tell you that if you clobber your son with that chair, then I'm going to have to arrest you."

Sonya was seething with anger. "You got yourself involved with drugs? Trevor, how could you be so stupid!"

"Just arrest me," Trevor demanded, pleading with Vance. He held his arms up, expecting a pair of handcuffs to be slapped on. "Please? Just do it and get it over with."

"We want information, Trevor," Captain Nelson snapped, causing the poor kid to jump. "Listen, you're small potatoes. There are bigger fish out there, namely the ones who gave you those drugs. They're the ones who deserve to be behind bars. Do you see what they've done there? This Skittles. We want him. We want Skittles' boss. They're the ones who have put all the risk on you. If something happens, and the drugs are discovered, which they have been, who is responsible? Right now, that's you. If you continue to sit there, tight-lipped, then that's what's gonna happen. You'll take the fall for all of this."

"Oh, he'll talk," Sonya promised. She fixed her son with a look. "Who gave that box to you? Out with it. Now. These nice officers have indicated they're not interested in you, but those other two. Spill."

"I'm no narc, Mom. I won't tell on my friends."

"Some friends they are," Sonya shot back, before anyone else could say anything. "They're relaxing at home while you're here, about to be arrested for possession of drugs. Is that what you want? You want to throw your life away like that? Have I not taught you better than that? Now, who gave you that box? It was Jay, wasn't it?"

After a few moments, Trevor reluctantly nodded.

"Now we're getting somewhere," Amanda said, pleased. "Captain, are you still there?"

"Present," Ryerson confirmed. "Please continue."

"Who was that?" Sonya asked.

"Captain of the Medford Police Department," Vance answered.

"Which sprinkles had the drugs?" Sonya asked. "Was it only the carob? What about the mocha? Wait. Were all of them drugs? I swear to God, Trevor, I'm gonna kill you. You made me a drug dealer!"

"Calm down, ma'am," Amanda soothed. "We need to know what Trevor knows. You can't kill him. Not yet, anyway."

Sonya smiled fleetingly before turning back to her son. "Is that why I can no longer find the box? Did you take it out of the pantry?"

"I had to give it back," Trevor whined. "You have no idea how mad they were when they saw how much you used. They knew they had to get it back.

They told me if I didn't tell them where it was, then I was going to get beat up."

"You told them I made ice cream with it," Sonya guessed.

"That's why Jillian's store was targeted," I said. "You told him about the nice lady from PV who bought a few tubs, right?"

"You're the one who broke into Mrs. Anderson's store?" Sonya shouted, as she lurched to her feet.

"I did no such thing!" Trevor insisted. "Skittles arranged for …"

"Don't stop now, kid," Captain Nelson said. "Skittles arranged for, what, to have a homeless person steal the ice cream?"

Trevor nodded again.

"Why trash the store?" I demanded. "Why didn't you just take the freakin' ice cream and go?"

"They had to hide their intentions," Amanda guessed. "And the second robbery?"

"It wasn't a robbery," I reminded her. "That kid, Barry Foster, said he bought the tubs." A thought occurred. I pulled out my phone and brought up the picture I took at the car wash, where Barry's face was clearly visible. "Recognize him?"

Everyone leaned forward to see the picture. Captain Nelson pulled a wire-rimmed set of reading glasses out from under his shirt and put them on.

"Yeah, I've seen him before," Trevor admitted. "What of it? What's he done?"

"Another recruit," Ryerson guessed, from the

cell phone's speaker.

"That's our thinking," Vance agreed.

"And then what, to throw off the police, the gang came in and trashed Vino's shop?" I guessed.

Trevor shrugged. "I dunno. I guess?"

"Who convinced you to join this gang?" Vance asked. "Was it your friend, Jay?"

"Skittles said a gang takes care of their own."

There was a loud smack, which made everyone jump, including the dogs. Sherlock even woofed a few times. Trevor yelped and was now rubbing the back of his head. His mother glared at him.

"Have I not given everything I have to make sure you're safe, fed, and have everything you need? Do you see your father doing anything like that? What in the world possessed you to agree to this?"

Trevor shrugged again. "I dunno."

"Omigod, I'm gonna kill my son," Sonya stated, as she started pacing behind the row of chairs facing the four of us. "You might as well lock me up. I watch TV. I know how to hide a body."

"Does he know who the leader is?" Ryerson asked.

Heads began nodding.

"That's a good question," Vance admitted. "What about it, Trevor? Who's in charge of the CL Crew?"

"I've never seen him up close," Trevor said. "I only ever dealt with Skittles."

"But you know it's a *him*," I said. "Do you have a

name?"

Trevor sighed. "Skittles calls him Roach. That's all I know."

As one, we all eyed one another. Roach? As in, a cockroach?

"Umm, are you sure about that?" I asked.

Trevor held out his right arm and pointed at his forearm. "He's got this huge cockroach tattooed, right here. So yeah, I'm pretty sure."

"I'll be damned," we heard Captain Ryerson say. "Cockroaches. I'm starting to see how your dogs' clues work."

"Zack," Vance suddenly said. "Why are Sherlock and Watson staring at the captain?"

"What's going on?" Ryerson wanted to know.

"Hold on," Nelson ordered. He turned to look at my dogs. Both were staring at him as though he had just opened a bag of doggie biscuits. "What's the matter, guys? Why are you looking at me?"

I suddenly pointed at the captain's chest. "Your glasses. More specifically, the dogs are looking at your eyeglass holders."

"My chain? What about it?"

Still holding my phone, I went back to the pictures and pulled up the shot from Corner Delights, which featured a pair of sunglasses dangling from a similar chain.

"That's him!" Trevor exclaimed, catching sight of my phone's display. "That's Roach!"

I looked at the picture. It was Tommaso! And, wouldn't you know it, he was wearing a black leather jacket. How had I not noticed that before?

I showed the picture to Vance. "Leather jacket, and he fits the description Captain Ryerson gave. Guys? There's our culprit!"

Vance sat back in his chair. "Remember what Vino said? When the dogs were staring at Tommaso? It was something about rearranging his nephew's face should he discover he had anything to do with what happened to his store."

"You're talking about the nephew of Vino Gasbardi?" Ryerson asked. "I'm putting out an APB, and I'm sending units over to Corner Delights right now."

"I hope you apprehend him without any incidents," I said.

"I'll keep everyone posted," Ryerson promised. "Cartez? All hands on deck. Get over there."

"Yes, sir!"

The line went dead. Amanda bade her goodbyes and hurried off.

"That wrapped itself up very nicely," Vance decided, pleased. He began collecting papers that were scattered across the table and returned them to the manila folder in front of him. "I'm with Zack. I hope we get this guy without incident."

"What about me?" Trevor nervously asked. "Am I free to go?"

"You're staying put until I find out we've got our man," the captain announced. He rose to his feet. "If those dogs are as good as I know they are, then this case will soon be wrapped up. Then, and only then, will you be cut loose."

"We will cooperate in whatever way we can," Sonya assured him. "Won't we."

The last comment was directed at her son, and I couldn't help but notice it wasn't phrased as a question.

I heard a whine and looked down at the dogs. Sherlock reared up on his hind legs, and placed his front paws on my leg. Recognizing the move as a request to be picked up, I lifted him to my lap. He proceeded to lick my arm for a few moments before settling down and resting his head on my left arm. The entire time, he was looking at Trevor.

"Why's he looking at me?" the boy complained. "I didn't do anything!"

Vance and I looked at each other before turning to study the teenager.

"Well, I did, but I already admitted to it. I didn't do anything else."

I looked down at Sherlock. A prickling sensation appeared in the back of my mind, and it wouldn't go away. I got the distinct impression that I was forgetting something. Again.

"Rainbows? Check."

"Cockroaches?"

Vance shuddered.

"Check. Eyeglass holders?" I continued. "Check."

Vance snapped his fingers. "Red backpacks?"

I looked at Trevor. "Any chance you own, or have worn, a red backpack recently?"

"No, of course not. What am I, twelve?"

"We must be interpreting that clue wrong," Vance decided.

Officers appeared at the door and escorted Trevor back to the holding cell. Sonya promised to wait in the lobby. She turned to us and thanked us for getting the police to work with her son and (hopefully) keep him out of jail.

As we were collecting our things, and heading for the parking lot, Vance's cell rang. "Detective Samuelson here. Detective Cartez, do you have good news? You don't? I'm sorry, that really … what's that? Absolutely. We're on our way."

"What's going on?" I asked, as I loaded the dogs into Vance's sedan. After all, Jillian had taken my Jeep home after dinner.

"Cartez is at Corner Delights. Tommaso is a no-show. Vino doesn't know where he is, and he's been absent for the better part of two days now. Cartez is hoping Sherlock and Watson will be able to shed some light on the matter."

I gotta tell you, I was really getting tired of looking at ice cream shops, especially this one. The day had been warm, and even though the sun had set several hours ago, business was booming for Corner Delights. Large groups of teenagers, some with sports cars, others with clunkers, were lining the parking lot. Also present were half a dozen police cars, which explained why all the kids were now watching, wide-eyed, from the safety of their cars.

"I've sent several units to his apartment," Amanda announced, the moment we exited our car. "He hasn't been home in a few days."

"He knows," Vance murmured. "He knows we've figured out who he is. He's lying low until all of this blows over. Well, it's up to us to figure out where he's gone."

"It's hopeless," Amanda argued. "Medford and the surrounding communities cover a lot of area. How can you possibly expect to find him now?"

I looked at the dogs and I had a flashback to Sitka, Alaska, where I realized not all of the corgi clues had been accounted for. Vance was right. We hadn't figured out *all* the clues.

"Red backpacks," I whispered.

Overhearing, Vance was suddenly staring at me. "That's the answer?"

"You said it earlier," I reminded my friend. "Red backpacks. We need to figure out its significance, and we need to do it now." Amanda was staring at me as though I had just started chanting in another language. "It happened to us up north just last week. Of all the corgi clues, the validity of one of them hasn't been determined. Red backpacks."

"That has got to be the mother of all long shots," Amanda complained.

"Maybe, but do you really want to risk ignoring it?" I countered.

"No. Your dogs have made a believer out of me. Very well, what do we do?"

A few of the local Medford police wandered over.

"The clue must refer to a location," I began. "We need to do some brainstorming, so let's hear it. I'll start. Is there a Red Backpack hotel?"

"None that I've heard of," Amanda said.

"Ditto," Vance agreed.

"What about a store by that name?" Amanda slowly asked.

I nodded. "That's a good guess. Let's see. This is where having a smart phone comes in. Let's check. Damn, this says there's no such business in the Medford area."

One policeman, a young guy who looked like he was fresh out of the police academy, raised his hand. He was probably around twenty, had short, buzzed blond hair, and striking blue eyes.

"You're asking about red backpacks?"

Detective Cartez looked up. "We are. Do you have something, Officer?"

"Well, I don't know if it's relevant, but I might. Up north, off of Crater Lake Highway, is a little place called Red Pack Deli. Maybe you've heard of it? They've got great cheesesteak sandwiches."

Amanda's eyes widened with shock. "I completely forgot about that. You're right! The four of you, get going! No lights, no sirens. We want to take them by surprise. Does anyone know when they close?"

"In about twenty minutes," Vance reported, holding up his own phone. "You guys had better move."

It only took ten. In ten short minutes, Medford cops had surrounded Red Pack Deli and took a very surprised, and completely furious, Tommaso Gasbardi into custody. The deli, we all learned later, was owned by Jessie Raymonds, father of one Jay Raymonds, otherwise known as Skittles. He had no idea what his son had become involved in, and once he saw the police stream through his door, he was quick to point out one of his son's friends was hiding in the back room.

The best part of the night, I'm sorry to say, happened nearly twenty minutes later. Vino, having been notified by the police, arrived at Red Pack Deli to confront his nephew. If you've never seen fear on a grown man's face, you should check out the pictures. Amanda was nice enough to photo-document the whole arrest. Tommaso couldn't get himself into a squad car fast enough.

EPILOGUE

Three months had passed. Jillian's newest venture, into frozen desserts, was (now) a huge success. In fact, Cookbook Nook's little café brought in so much business that Jillian had hired an architect for design ideas in order to expand her café. Why? That was because of her new secret weapon. My wife had hired Sonya Ladd to oversee all food operations. Also, not wanting the poor woman to commute nearly a full hour every single day, my wife arranged for her newest employee to move to PV.

True to their word, Captains Nelson and Ryerson were able to keep Trevor out of jail. After all, the entire CL Crew had been disbanded, and poor Tommaso wouldn't be seeing the light of day anytime soon. Surprisingly, Vino's nephew copped to both killings, stating he hadn't wanted to do either, but was desperate to reclaim the sprinkles that were never supposed to be used.

With regard to the wager between police departments, it was obviously determined PV had won, but Captain Nelson had wisely decided to forgo the consequences in favor of fostering better relations with their much larger neighbor. Captain Ryerson wouldn't go on record with any type of statement, but we heard from Cartez, who said her captain admitted he owed PV a favor, and apparently, that was good enough for Captain Nelson.

At the moment, Jillian and I, along with the dogs, were standing in front of our newly completed home. Judging from the size of our new house, I really should start referring to it as a mansion, because that was the only accurate way to describe it.

At three stories high, not including a basement, *Corgi Crossing* looked like it belonged on the grounds of an elegant French estate. I may be biased when I say this, but I think, hands down, it's the nicest house in PV. Like the name? Jillian and I hadn't come to a mutual decision until the day we closed on the house and picked up our keys. As much as I wanted to name it after one of my favorite movies, or books, or even characters, I really wanted a name that personified us. *Corgi Crossing* did exactly that. I feel like a couple of corgis crossed our paths, and because of them, we became a family. So, the name stuck.

As for our new home, its list of features could put practically any house to shame. Theater, indoor pool, library, you name it. And, if you recall, I specifically had so many secret doors and hidden passages installed that it'd put Highland House to shame. And, they would remain secret from all but the two of us. Well, four, if you included Sherlock and Watson.

I've always said I'm nothing more than a big kid at heart. Well, this is where he definitely came out to play. If you were to go down the stairs and visit the bottom floor of our mansion, you'll discover my pride and joy.

I brought in retro arcade machines from all across the country. Everything from Donkey Kong to Frogger found a home in my game room. Turns out Jillian liked playing the old arcade machines just as much as I did. She also ended up offering the best suggestion yet. Skee ball. Know what that is? I ended up reaching out to several large pizza franchises, you know, the ones with a large rodent as a mascot? Anyway, they ended up selling me a few machines, so they were now in my collection as well.

Now, let me stop for a moment and let you in on something. I know what you're thinking. Why waste so much money on something as impractical as a full-sized arcade room? That's easy. I spent huge chunks of my childhood in mall arcades. I'd blow my entire allowance trying to master certain games. I should also mention that you won't find a single arcade cabinet from the '90s. Eighties and late '70s only, please. Why? Well, that's when I played these games. I'm not interested in the mass destruction of the newer video games. I don't care about playing online shoot-em-ups. If I'm going to kill something, let it be a frog as I try to get it to cross the road without being flattened by speeding cars.

The only reason I tell you all of this is to set the scene for what was about to happen.

"It's looking quite nice down here," my wife observed, after my latest cabinet had been installed. "Is that an actual Pac-Man cabinet?"

"Found it in Idaho. Yet another arcade going belly-up."

"Their loss, your gain. Do you know what this room needs?"

I looked around the large open area, taking in everything one would expect to find in an older arcade: bright lights, neon signs, and the plush arm chairs situated practically everywhere.

"And what would that be?"

"Memorabilia. Knickknacks. You say you're a *Star Wars* fan, yet if you look around, I don't see anything. How can you look at yourself in a mirror?"

"Oh, it's coming. My *Star Wars* collection is sitting inside a number of crates inside the theater, out of the way. I'm trying to figure out the best way to display them. Maybe you could give me some ideas?"

Jillian beamed a smile. "I'd love to. Hey, did you know Medford will be hosting its first Comic-Con in at least four years?"

About ready to play a game of Robotron, I looked over at my wife. "Really? How cool is that? I can only hope they bring some people in that I've actually heard of, not someone from a show I've never watched."

"I can guarantee you've heard of their headliner. He's been in several of your favorite movies."

"Sure, sure. Hit me with your best."

"Lieutenant Coffee, from *Abyss*. Corporal Hicks, from *Aliens*. Johnny Ringo, from *Tombstone*, and of course, Kyle Reese, from the original *Terminator*. Do any of those names ring a bell?"

"Don't play with me, lady," I mock-warned. "I know full well who you're talking about. You can't possibly be suggesting Michael Biehn will be visiting Medford?"

"He'll be here in less than two months," Jillian confirmed. "He'll be signing autographs, taking pictures, and talking about his favorite characters that he's portrayed over the years. Interested in going? It says here that the tickets will go on sale next week."

"Oh, abso-freakin'-lutely! Count me in! I'd love to meet the guy."

Not only would I get to meet an actual celebrity, I never would have guessed that he would become an impromptu partner of mine, and good friend, as he assisted me for several days as he helped me search.

Search for what, you ask? Oh, just something that has actual screen time in one of the most iconic sci-fi movies of all time. Naturally, it had to be stolen while he was in my neck of the woods.

To be continued! Zack and the dogs will return in Case of the Hobbit Heist!

AUTHOR'S NOTE

I hope you enjoyed the story! For those of you familiar with the southern Oregon area, you'll no doubt recognize street names, and an occasional business. However, I've changed most of the names, just in case people don't want to see their names in print.

I'm trying to keep everyone evolving. Let's face it, as time goes on, nothing really stays the same. Cookbook Nook is expanding, more employees are being brought in, and in Zack and Jillian's case, new homes are constructed. I found the house plans for Corgi Crossing online and have them printed out and taped to a wall next to my desk. All those rooms that I mentioned aren't fabricated, but actually exist. Game room, theater, theatre (with the *r* in a different spot), indoor pool, and on and on. Who wouldn't want to live in a place like that?

Those eagle-eyed readers might've noticed a little nod toward my Tales of Lentari fantasy series. I've been toying with the idea of a cross-over, and as such, I'm sending out some feelers to see what people would say. I started with the name of the winery, the bas-relief in Highland House, and now this. No promises, but I will say that, if you'd like to see a story that has the characters of Corgi Case Files meeting up with those in my Tales of Lentari series, drop me a line, leave a comment on my blog, or let me know via social media. The more interest I get, the more inclined I'll become to give it a try.

What's next for Zack and the gang? Well, a comic-con is going to show up in nearby Medford, the first time in a couple of years. Naturally, things don't go so well. There's a robbery of a screen-used prop from a very famous movie. And, well, there might be a new friendship forming between Zack and the owner of that prop, who just so happened to star in the aforementioned famous movie. *Case of the Hobbit Heist* will be released later this year!

Meanwhile, catch up on the entire
Corgi Case Files Series
Available in e-book and paperback

If you enjoy Epic Fantasy, check out Jeff's other series:
BAKKIAN CHRONICLES
The Prophecy
Insurrection
Amulet of Aria
Disneyland Debacle (short story)
Winter Wonderland (short story)

TALES OF LENTARI
Lost City
Something Wyverian This Way Comes
A Portal for Your Thoughts
Thoughts for A Portal
Wizard in the Woods
Close Encounters of the Magical Kind
The Hunt for Red Oskorlisk (short story)

JEFFREY POOLE

May the Fang be With You (Pirates trilogy #1)
The Hammer is Strong with This One (Pirates #2)
These are Not the Stones You're Looking For (Pirates #3)
Blast from the Past

DRAGONS OF ANDELA
Harness the Fire
Strike the Spark
Clear the Water*

Made in the USA
Middletown, DE
01 September 2024

60171833R00165